One Little Question
A Steamy Ensemble Romantic Comedy
Cheryl Terra

bang it out
WRITING

Bang It Out Writing

CONTENT WARNINGS

Please note that this books is written in Canadian English, which has rules and spellings from both UK and US English.

While not a dark romance, this book covers some heavier topics. I have tried to reflect those here as best I can without providing spoilers, but if you have concerns about any of the items listed and wish to know more, please reach out to me via email at **info@cherylterra.com**.

As a steamy romance, this book is intended for mature adults. There are multiple sexually explicit scenes and profanity. Some scenes include mild/light instances of Dominant/submissive dynamics, choking, honorifics, face sitting, and other sexual actions.

While lighthearted, there are discussions of heavier topics that may be triggering for some readers, including body confidence issues/internalized fatphobia and discussion of diet culture, childhood illnesses such as cancer (mild/offscreen situation), sexual harassment (mild/offscreen situation), and pregnancy (featuring already-pregnant characters/discussions of having children).

CHAPTER ONE

Jay

OF ALL THE MESSAGES I was expecting my wife to send me that day, that was not one of them.

Not that she never sent me... you know. *Risqué* sorts of messages. I'd opened my share of unexpected tit pics in the middle of drinks with the guys, subtly tilting my phone away from everyone else and indulging in the sight of her perfect brown skin and enticing cleavage and dark, puffy nipples. And then I'd try to finish my beer as fast as I could before rushing home so I could get my mouth around one of those beautiful nipples.

What could I say? Candice knew how to get me going. It wasn't *the* reason I'd married her, but I wasn't going to sit there and pretend like my wife wasn't hot as fuck.

But she hadn't sent me a picture of her tits. Or her ass. Or, like when I was a very, very lucky man, her pussy. This was just a question and a couple of emojis. It wasn't even that suggestive.

The thing was, I knew where she was.

And I knew who she was with.

And so did the rest of the guys on my crew.

"What's got your face so red, Jay-Jay?" asked Seth loudly.

"Nothing," I said. "And stop calling me that. Don't think I won't get you fired, new boy."

Seth mocked my words, a grin spreading across his face as he stripped his work gloves off and rolled the cuffs of his coveralls up. He was the baby of the crew and looked it, though in fairness, that's just because the rest of us looked old as balls.

Well, except Rob. And Adrian. And Kendra was only two years older than Seth and would've slapped me for saying she looked old at twenty-seven. And Benny didn't actually *look* old as balls. He just seemed it because he was the only one with kids.

It was me, okay? I looked old as balls. Forty was going to hit me three days after Christmas, but I'd been going grey for ten years by that point and working with a crew who was all younger than me made me distinctly aware of the fact that I was the fucking *adult* on the team.

Which had to be dangerous, but there we were.

Candice didn't seem to mind how I looked, though, and that was all that mattered. She liked it, she said, the grey beard on my chin and the fact that the salt had taken over my salt-and-pepper hair. Her favourite thing, she said, was when I got home from work and still had my sunglasses on, the sleeves of my coveralls rolled up to my elbows.

"You grime down real good, baby," she would say. "Not that you don't clean up real nice, but I like you a little dirty."

And even though it was just a couple of days before Christmas and the snow was flying, I always made sure I had my sunglasses on and my sleeves rolled up when I got home from the site every day.

I wondered if Laura, Seth's little teacher girlfriend, liked him grimed down too. Damn kid was too good-looking for his own fucking good. If I had looks like that when I was fifteen years younger... well, actually, I would've done fuck all differently, since I would've already met my wife and that woman had me hooked from day one.

But Seth was the kind of guy with a smile that made girls' hearts melt, even if he did need to grow up a little. When I first hired him, I had said it would just be a seasonal thing. He was a little too party animal, a little too misguided, a little too *young*. But I think, mostly, all of that was because he was just a little lost. All it took was a few weeks of guidance and tough love before he'd started changing, and the kid had ended up fitting in pretty well. So I'd decided to keep him on the crew.

"How are you not freezing?" Seth asked, staring at Benny, who was undoing his winter coat and fanning himself off.

"Working harder than you, probably," Benny said, and everyone chuckled even though Seth was right. How Benny was sweating when it was below freezing and we were in the middle of rough framing a house for some rich fuck who was paying out the ass for his new mansion to be constructed as fast as possible was beyond me. I was working my ass off just like the rest of them, but my toes were frozen between my steel-toes and I was almost regretting calling a coffee break, since at least when I was moving, it wasn't so damn cold.

That, and I wouldn't have seen that little question from Candice.

Why do you need to know that? I messaged back, then tucked my phone back in my coverall pocket before taking a swig from the coffee Adrian had just brought to the site.

"Seth's got a point," Kendra said to me as she leaned against the skeleton of a wall we'd gotten up that morning and ran a hand through her short, shaggy brown hair. "C'mon, boss-man. You're making us work the whole fuckin' weekend. Entertain us a bit. What kinda message did you just get?"

I gave her a stern look. "I didn't make you do shit. You know Dave's the one who told the client we'd have it done before Christmas. I'm stuck working this weekend just like the rest of you sorry fucks."

"Yeah," Rob said as he helped himself to a coffee, shivering as he took his glove off so he could pop it open. "Dave's the fuckin' Scrooge, not Jay."

I nodded at him gratefully. Rob was thirty and had been working on the crew with me for coming up on ten years already. I might've been Dave's second in command, but Rob was *my* right-hand guy. The dude was intimidating: nearly six and a half feet tall with what looked like half his yearly income inked onto his white skin, from the top of his neck to the backs of his hands and probably on his legs too, plus a shaved bald head and a dark, trimmed goatee.

But Rob was a teddy bear, just like most gigantic dudes with broad shoulders and dark, intimidating eyes tended to be. And he was loyal as all fuck. I hadn't asked him yet, but I had a feeling when Dave finally fucking retired, Rob would go in with me on buying the business. I hoped so, anyway.

"It's not so bad," Benny said. "We finish today and tomorrow, then a week off for the holidays? Paid? It was pretty nice of Dave to do that."

"It was," Seth agreed. "Laura's excited, too. Since she's off for Christmas break from the school and she's not going home this year."

"Exactly," Benny continued. "And besides, I'm taking all the overtime I can get. Christmas bills aren't gonna pay themselves, and my boys wanted one of those new fucking Nintendos this year."

"Shut the fuck up with your common sense over there, Benny," Kendra said.

"And your kids wanted a PlayStation, not a Nintendo," Seth added.

Benny was a great dude. He was a couple of years younger than me and the only dad of the group, at least for now. Candice and I had decided early on that we didn't want kids, but I had a feeling Rob would be getting started on that whole thing pretty soon, once he finally wifed Halle. And who knew about Seth, but he had lots of time to figure that out.

Though, Kendra and her wife had finally found a sperm donor they both agreed on, so her wife was pregnant and due in the next couple of months. I guess she wasn't technically a *dad*, but she was part of the crew.

But for now, Benny was the crew dad and had the bod to show it. Not that it bothered him; the second anyone joked about his dad bod, he reminded us he had proof he'd gotten laid at least twice—though he was gonna be able to change the count on that pretty soon—and what the fuck did we have except our word for it?

Then someone would respond with something like, "Well, Benny, most people don't need proof, but I guess when you're pale as a sheet of paper and have red hair and ginger scruff on your face that you refuse to shave, you kinda have something to prove."

The rest of the crew was still laughing at Benny when my phone buzzed again. I tried to subtly take it out of my pocket to see what Candice had replied with.

Which was dumb of me.

Because the girls and I are trying to figure it out and you've got a whole crew right there to ask, said her message.

I gritted my teeth as I typed a quick response. *Yeah, a whole crew... of THEIR partners. This isn't anonymous at all.*

"Is it nudes?" Kendra asked, suddenly beside me.

"Huh?" I said, jerking my phone away.

The crew roared with laughter.

"Is Candice sending you nudes?" she repeated. "And more importantly, can I see them? Your wife's hot."

"They're not nudes," I repeated. "And fuck you. I'm not letting you see my wife naked. And *what* makes you think I'm getting nudes right now, anyway?"

"'Cause you've got that 'I just saw something real naughty' look on your face."

I rolled my eyes. "That's not a thing. I don't have a look for that."

"Oh, Jay McJacobson, you totally do," Adrian said. He was a short guy in his late twenties with light brown skin, thick eyebrows, and a total shit-disturber attitude. "It's kinda like you're trying to hold something in. Easy to mistake for your 'I got the shits and someone's in the porta-john' face, though. The coffee run through you that fast already?"

"You're sick, man," I said.

"Wait, Candice is sending you nudes?" Seth asked, frowning. "The fuck kind of cookie exchange is your wife hosting?"

"Cookie exchange?" Adrian repeated. "The fuck's a cookie exchange?"

"They all bake a bunch of cookies and trade them," Rob said. "Halle made her mint Oreo meltaways again. I swear to God, if I had to pick a last meal, it would be those."

"Candice invited Denise, Benny, but she said couldn't get a sitter," I said. "You know she could've brought the boys, right?"

"Yeah, totally," Benny said. "She was planning on going to see her mom today with the boys, though. Help her parents get ready for Christmas sort of thing."

Kendra snorted. "How'd you know about the cookie exchange, Seth?"

His cheeks turned pink. "Candice was nice enough to invite Laura after they met at the Christmas party last weekend."

The crew *ooo*ed.

"Ah shit, man," Adrian groaned. "It's that serious already? Now I'm the only single fucker here."

"I wasn't single before," Seth said. "Laura and I have been dating for, like, six months."

"Yeah, but you aren't married," Kendra said.

"Neither is Rob," I said.

"Might as well be," Adrian grumbled, then sighed. "Well, congrats, Seth. You're officially part of the crew. Your girl's in the wives' club."

"It's not a wives' club," Rob said. "It's a small town and they like to welcome new people. And since Dave is making us work all weekend to finish the framing, they decided to amuse themselves with a cookie exchange."

"Which brings me back to my original point," Seth said. "Why is Candice sending you nudes from a *cookie exchange*?"

"She's not sending me nudes!" I said.

"Boo," Kendra muttered.

My phone picked that moment to buzz again. I tried to ignore it, but everyone's eyes were on me. Sighing, I looked down at the new message from Candice.

That makes them the perfect group to ask, her message said. *Come on, baby. It's just one little question. Ask for me and I'll let you do it when you get home tonight.*

It was that more than anything which made me cave. I mean, she would've let me do it anyway. But still.

"If you gotta go to the john so you can take a pic to send back, we'll give you a few minutes," Adrian said.

The crew chuckled again and I sighed.

"Alright, assholes," I said. "You wanna know what the message said?"

"Nah, we changed our minds," Benny said. "'Course we want to know."

I took a deep breath, then let it out.

"Candice said the girls want to know if guys go down on women for the woman's pleasure, or is it because the guy gets off on it."

CHAPTER TWO

Laura

"JAY GETS OFF ON eating pussy."

My fingers tightened so hard around the stem of my champagne glass that I was almost afraid it would snap. Luckily, every other woman in the room cackled with laughter, so no one seemed to notice my startled reaction.

The last thing I'd expected to be talking about at a cookie exchange with a group of women I knew solely from the workplace Christmas party my boyfriend had taken me to a week ago was sex. Not that I was some kind of prude or something. I just... well. I mean, I barely knew any of them. And Candice was Jay's wife. And from what Seth had said, Jay was kind of like his boss. Not his boss-boss, but the supervisor of the crew. The boss-boss didn't show up at the builds or something like that.

So basically, my boyfriend's boss's wife was sitting there telling every single person in the room that her husband *really* liked eating pussy.

And the whole thing had started because of Halle's cookies.

Candice had explained the cookie exchange rules to me over a few glasses of wine at the Christmas party. Eight dozen cookies, she'd said: one dozen for each of the other people attending, plus one for yourself, and one for all of us to enjoy while we were drinking mimosas at her place the following Saturday. And while I wasn't a *huge* fan of baking, I could make a pretty decent rum ball and I didn't have a ton of friends in Southbush, so I agreed to it.

The joy of moving to a small town to take a teaching job, I guess.

Thankfully, I'd met Seth almost immediately after moving here. Well, re-met, I guess. We'd run into each other at the grocery store and realized we'd met at a club in Calgary a few years earlier.

And by "met," I mean made out.

Then left the club together and went to my place.

Then hooked up.

Then hooked up again when we woke up the next morning.

Then texted a few times and talked about meeting up again, but he wasn't actually from Calgary—he'd said he was from a small town an hour or so north—so things had just never quite worked out. Which was sad, because it had been fun. Not that I'd expected it to turn into anything more. I might not have done the whole one-night-stand thing very often, but I didn't think it had to be anything more than a good time.

Even if the guy was *gorgeous*, like Seth was. Dirty blond hair, broad shoulders, one of those bright and genuine smiles that made everyone else want to smile with him. And he worked a pretty physical job, so he also had a super nice body. So running into him randomly in what turned out to be his hometown had been... well.

Really great.

We'd been dating ever since, but I hadn't met a ton of other friends in Southbush. So when Candice invited me to the cookie exchange, I jumped at the chance to connect with other women.

They were all a bit older than me, but that was okay. It wasn't like I was a child; I was twenty-four, with a career and an apartment and had moved from Calgary to Southbush all by myself. So I figured that made me pretty mature. And I knew I looked a little older than I actually was; that was purposeful, since it made the students and parents I taught respect me a bit more.

After all, if the high school kids I taught found out I was only a few years older than them, they'd probably use that against me. I already had a problem with the older boys thinking it was okay to hit on me, and worse, with certain parents thinking it was *my* fault.

"Well, maybe you shouldn't spend so much time making yourself up for school," one mom had said when I let her know her son had tried to grab my ass during biology.

I'd looked down at my outfit, which was a collared navy-blue polka dot dress with a skirt that hit just below my knees. And I had leggings on underneath it. I mean, sure, I'd curled my dark brown hair and I was wearing a bit of makeup—just a pale pink lip gloss and some mascara to highlight my brown eyes—but I'd hardly call that *making myself up*.

And regardless, my clothing didn't give teenage boys the right to grope me. Nor did the fact that we all knew what she was actually talking about, which was that my boobs were too big.

Because they were. Not big enough that they bothered me or anything, but with a slim waist and somewhat flat hips, I had a top-heavy sort of look that I couldn't do a whole heck of a lot about. So even though I wasn't showing off my boobs, they were just... there.

Seth had been livid when I told him about the boy who tried to grab me, especially when I said the administration's solution had been to switch him out of my biology class... but had kept him in my chemistry class. But after Seth had popped by with Rob, his larger-than-life coworker who would've only looked out of place in a motorcycle club because he could dwarf a Harley, to pick me up from the school one day, that student had surprisingly kept his hands to himself for the rest of the semester.

I still made an effort to look older and frumpier than I was, though. Just in case.

I wasn't sure how old Candice was. I thought she might be in her mid-thirties since her husband, Jay, had lamented about how he was turning forty at the Christmas party the previous week and she'd told him it didn't matter because he could still pull a hot young thing like her. Her sense of humour and quick wit had made me like Candice immediately. She was a Black woman with a coy smile and sparkling eyes beneath her coiled hair. As soon as Seth had introduced me at the party, she'd taken me under her wing, introducing me to the other people and making sure I felt like part of the group.

Halle had been one of those people. She was Rob's... something. *Girlfriend* felt like the wrong word since I knew they'd been together for five years, but they weren't married. She was absolutely beautiful in the Punk Rock Princess Barbie kind of way. She was in her early thirties and had the longest, blondest hair I'd ever seen on anyone. There were a bunch of piercings in her ears and a hoop in her nose and just like Rob, she was covered in tattoos. I'd seen a few of them at the Christmas party when Halle had been wearing a shiny green dress with thin straps, but at the cookie exchange, she was wearing a horribly ugly Christmas sweater with the characters from *The Muppet Christmas Carol* on it, so most of them were covered.

The other women I'd only just met that day. Nadia, a neighbour of Candice's who had made incredible Indian cookies that she refused to share the recipe for because she said her grandmother had brought it over when she immigrated. Then Trish, Candice's sister-in-law that worked at the library with Phoebe, who was probably the closest to my age. She was a larger woman and looked adorable in a cozy fair-isle patterned sweater dress that clung to her curves. Her legs were crossed over each other as she sat on the arm of the sofa, insisting to Candice that she was more comfortable there. With rosy white skin and shiny black hair, she almost looked like a pin-up version of Snow White. She was quiet and had a dry sense of humour that kept us all laughing.

Especially after she commented on Halle's mint Oreo meltaway cookies.

"Oh, my *God*," Candice said after taking a first bite of the cookie. "Halle, these are fantastic."

"Um, yeah," said Trish. "These are... wow. *Wow*."

"These are the kind of cookies a guy would go down on you for," Phoebe said in her soft voice.

We all burst out laughing.

"Well, we all know what Rob's doing tonight," Nadia said.

"You know it." There was a tightness to Halle's smile and a fake brightness in her voice. "So, the key to making them that kind of melt-in-your-mouth is—"

"Uh-uh, nope," Candice interrupted. "What's wrong, Halle?"

Halle tried to look innocent, which failed given the whole "punk rock princess" part of her look. "What? Why would something be wrong?"

"Um, because Nadia just made a joke about oral sex and you got all tense about it," Trish said. "What's wrong?"

"Does Rob not go down?" Candice asked bluntly. "Do I gotta make Jay have a talk with him?"

"Oh my God," Halle said. "No, of course not. He does. He's not one of those losers who refuses to."

I shifted uncomfortably in my seat and sipped my mimosa.

"But?" Candice pressed. "Come on. You know you can say anything. This is a safe space."

"There's nothing to say," Halle replied. "Really."

"Do you not like it?" Trish asked.

"No, I... I do."

"Oh," Phoebe said.

We all looked at her, which she didn't seem to expect. Her cheeks flushed pink and she looked at Halle apologetically.

"He's just not very good at it, is he?" Phoebe asked.

Halle's entire face went red. "He's... he's... I mean, he..."

"Oh, *no*," Nadia said, trying not to laugh.

"... he tries," Halle said, her voice high-pitched.

Immediately, a look of regret spread across her face. There was a beat of silence, then we all burst out laughing again.

Well, except Halle.

CHAPTER THREE

Laura

"DON'T TELL HIM I said that," Halle begged, devastation on her face as the rest of us tried to contain our giggles. "Please. He just doesn't seem to *get* what he needs to do, but he really likes doing it."

"You have to communicate with him," Trish argued. "You deserve to have good sex."

"I *do* have good sex," Halle said fiercely. "Have you seen my man?"

"I have always wondered how he doesn't crush your pelvis when you two fuck," Candice said.

Halle smacked her hands to her hips. "These child-bearing hips are good for a lot more than bringing rugrats into the world."

I started laughing so hard mimosa came out of my nose and Nadia hurriedly passed me a napkin as the rest of the room cracked up.

"Look, it's not a big deal," Halle said when we'd calmed down again. "This is just like... like *one* thing that isn't great. Trust me, the rest of our sex life is just..." She bit her lip, then shook her head. "He loves doing it anyway, so it's more for him than it is for me, and that's fine."

"Why would it be for him?" Phoebe asked.

We all chuckled again, but Phoebe didn't seem to be joking that time. She glanced down at her drink uncertainly.

"Wait, are you saying Miguel doesn't enjoy it?" Halle asked.

"Who's Miguel?" I asked.

"Phoebe's boyfriend," Trish said. "He's a bartender at Whisky Sours."

Phoebe shrugged. "I don't know if he likes it. But I... I don't, really."

"*What*?!" at least three people said in shock.

"Why not?" Candice asked, bewildered.

Phoebe's face turned fully red. "I just don't. And Miguel doesn't press for it, so it's just... like, some guys just don't enjoy it, probably?"

"Every guy I've ever been with has loved going down on me," Halle said. "I swear, they're more into it than I am half the time."

"Jay gets off on eating pussy," Candice said, which was when I nearly broke my champagne flute.

"Well, Jay is weird," Phoebe said.

"No, he's not!" Candice replied. "Halle just said Rob does, too."

"Anthony only does it because I like it," Trish said.

"Okay, first of all: ew," Candice said. "I do not want to hear that about my brother. Second of all, *what*?! He doesn't like doing it?"

"If I didn't ask for it, he wouldn't do it." Trish shrugged. "But he does it. I don't think I'd ever have dated a guy who wouldn't go down on me."

Nadia shook her head. "I'm on Phoebe's side. I don't like it."

"But does Scott still want to do it?" Trish asked.

Nadia shrugged. "Sometimes. But he knows it's not going to get me off."

"Okay, so Rob and Jay are into it," Candice said. "Scott too, probably. Miguel is a question mark and—" she shuddered "—my brother is neutral. So the real question is, do guys go down on women because *women* like it? Or is even *this* all about the man's pleasure?"

"What about Seth?" Halle said, looking at me.

My heart thudded in my chest. "What about him?"

She raised her eyebrows. "Have you been listening to the conversation? Does Seth go down on you because you like it or because *he* likes it?"

It would have been so easy to just say I didn't like it. But I could feel everyone's eyes on me and I panicked. My mouth felt dry, but my mimosa was empty and more alcohol probably wouldn't have helped anyway. Instead, I cleared my throat and tried not to make eye contact with anyone.

"Um, no," I said.

There was silence in the room.

"No as in... as in he *doesn't* like it?" Trish said.

"Or no as in he doesn't *do* it?" Halle asked.

I opened my mouth, then closed it for a moment before speaking. "Some guys just don't like to do that and that's—"

"No *way*!" Candice shouted, making me jump. "Oh my God, Laura, are you saying Seth doesn't go down on you at all?!"

"If she doesn't like it, that's not a big deal," Phoebe said quietly.

"But then she would have said that," Candice said. "Seriously, Laura. Is Seth the kind of guy that insists on blowjobs but won't go down on a woman?"

"He is not," I said indignantly. "He just doesn't like to do that and I don't... it's not that big a deal to me."

And that was the truth.

Sort of.

I mean, I did kind of wish he'd do it, but it was one of those things that Seth *really* didn't like. And it wasn't like he demanded blowjobs. I mean, I did give them to him, but a big part of it was because *I* liked doing that. If I didn't want to do it, he would've respected that. Just like I respected him not wanting to go down on me. I didn't know why he didn't want to do it, and that was okay.

Our sex life was perfectly fine without that.

Mostly.

"I didn't think he seemed like that type of guy," Halle said.

"What type of guy?" I asked.

"You know," Trish said, looking apologetic. "Like, too good to go down on someone. It's just... I don't know. Kind of selfish, I guess."

"He is not selfish!" I said. "It's not that big a deal."

"How is it not a big deal?" Candice asked, bewildered. "I mean, I just don't get it. I love it when Jay goes down on me."

I shrugged helplessly. "It just… it just isn't. Please don't… don't bother him about it. He'd be embarrassed if he knew I said anything and he really isn't… I mean, you're judging him for no reason. Please don't."

Candice looked like she was about to argue, but something on my face must have stopped her. Instead, she stood up and grabbed my mimosa glass, bringing it to the island in the kitchen and busying herself refilling my glass, as well as hers.

"Well, either way, this has settled fuck all," she said as she poured orange juice into the glasses. "We aren't any closer to figuring out whether guys go down for their pleasure or their woman's pleasure."

"I think it's probably a mix of both," Nadia said.

"But I mean, do you go down on a guy for your pleasure or his?" Trish asked. "Because like, I don't know many women who are all 'oh, I totally get off on giving head,' but—"

"I totally get off on giving head," Candice said, and the room dissolved into laughter again. But I was thankful she said it, partly so I didn't have to say it and partly because I was kind of relieved I wasn't weird for enjoying it.

And also a bit so that I didn't have to get more into the things that I enjoyed with these women I barely knew. Like how I secretly loved using my breasts to get guys off. Because yeah, I didn't love all the attention they got me all of the time, but I did kind of love how mesmerized Seth got by them. I loved having them touched and squeezed and the way he'd get distracted when they bounced or swung when we were having sex.

My theory was that I was so used to my chest causing me trouble in real life—like being judged or shamed simply because they were *there*—that it was kind of nice for them to be appreciated, you know? But I didn't really want to get into that with everyone in the room.

"Okay, but like, in general," Trish said when we'd calmed down again. "Most guys are totally into getting blowjobs. I'd wager that it's not *as* common for women to do it solely because they like it. So how common is it for a guy to do it because he enjoys it versus doing it because he... you know. Like..."

"Tolerates it?" Halle finished, and Trish nodded.

Candice returned to the table, her eyes sparkling as she passed me a mimosa before taking her seat.

"Only one way to find out," she said.

"What's that?" Phoebe asked.

Candice took a sip of her drink, then pulled her phone out of her pocket.

"Simple. Let's ask the men."

CHAPTER FOUR
Rob

"I GET OFF ON going down on women," Kendra said.

"You, Kendra McKendraington?" Adrian said, feigning shock. "Preposterous! Does your wife know about this?"

She punched him in the arm. "Let me guess. You're too good to get your tongue all up in there with all your fuckin' one-night stands."

He snorted. "Are you kidding? I fucking *love* it. Just because she's a one-night stand doesn't mean I don't go out of my way to get her off. I'm not a douchebag."

"Guess you have to have something going for you, short stuff," Jay said.

Adrian flipped him off. "I pull way more pussy than any of you."

"Your Fleshlight doesn't count," Benny said.

Adrian flipped him off too, but he was laughing.

"Okay, but are you going down on her for *her*?" I asked. "Or are you doing it for you?"

"Yes," Adrian replied.

"For her," Benny said.

I was almost pleased to see that multiple people turned to Benny with indignation on their face.

"Seriously, man?" asked Jay, his thick eyebrows furrowing. "You're not into it?"

Benny shrugged, not at all embarrassed as he ran a hand through his thick ginger hair. "I don't hate it, but it doesn't do much for me. I like that she likes it."

"Well, at least you're still doing it," Adrian said.

"Probably be divorced if I wasn't," Benny said. "She asks me to do it, I do it. And I guess I do alright at it because she keeps asking for it, so I'm not gonna complain. Me eating her pussy means I'm about to get laid."

"How did this even come up?" Seth interrupted, his face uncharacteristically serious.

"You put a group of women in a room with hundreds of Christmas cookies and a ton of mimosas, and you're wondering why they're talking about sex?" Kendra asked. "Jeez, Seth. Are you a virgin or something?"

He glared at Kendra, but didn't say anything.

"Apparently Halle made 'the kind of cookies a guy would go down on you for,'" Jay said, reading off his phone before glancing up at me. "You need cookies to go down on her?"

"Oh, fuck off," I said, though I was laughing along with everyone. "The cookies are a bonus. Halle gets eaten out whenever I want it. Which is *always*. She doesn't even *have* to ask for it."

"Good man," Kendra said.

"Okay, so that's three votes for 'guys enjoy eating pussy,'" Jay said.

"But Benny said he doesn't," Seth said.

Jay fixed an unimpressed stare on the younger man.

"What?" Seth said.

"Rob, Adrian, and *me*," Jay replied, and Seth's face went even redder than it had been as he ran a hand through his short, blond hair.

"I didn't say I didn't enjoy it," Benny said loudly. "Just that I do it for her, not for me."

"Do I seriously not get a vote?" Kendra asked.

"Fine," Jay said, rubbing a hand along his greying beard. "Four votes for getting off on eating pussy, two for doing it because she asks for it. I'll let Candice know."

"Don't say who's who," Adrian said. "Nadia's over there and this is *not* something I need my sister knowing about me."

"Wait, Seth didn't actually vote," Benny said.

I snorted. "If he got off on it, he would've said it right away. Right, new boy?"

"I... yeah," Seth said, but his voice was uncertain.

The crew went quiet. Benny and I exchanged a look, then Benny glanced at Jay, who raised his eyebrows at Seth.

"Oh my God," Adrian said slowly. "You don't go down on Laura, do you?"

"That's none of your fucking business," Seth said, pulling his work gloves on and refusing to look at anyone.

"Seriously?" Kendra said, her eyes round.

"Dude, what the hell?" Adrian said.

"What do you do when she asks for it?" Benny said.

"Is the coffee break over yet?" Seth asked pointedly.

"Nope," Jay said, sipping his coffee and leaning casually against one of the studs. "So why don't you eat your girlfriend's pussy, Seth?"

Seth glared at him. "She doesn't ask for it."

"I mean, do you ask her for blowjobs?" I asked.

"What? No," he said.

"But do you *get* blowjobs?"

His jaw twitched, but he didn't respond.

"Her not asking doesn't mean she doesn't *want* it," I said. "Halle doesn't ask for it much either."

Seth glared at me. "So how do you know she even wants it, then?"

"I feel like we've touched a little nervey-nerve," Kendra said in a mocking, high-pitched tone. "Are you sure Laura doesn't want it, Seth?"

He threw his hands up, his frustration finally snapping. "I don't like it, okay? I don't like going down on her."

"On her, or in general?" Jay asked, his voice almost sympathetic.

Seth couldn't meet anyone's eyes. "Anyone. I don't like it. And it's never been an issue. Laura doesn't ask me to do it. So I don't know why I'm listening to you assholes make fun of me for it."

"Because we care about you, buddy." Adrian went over to Seth and threw an arm around his shoulders. "And last I heard, little bitches who don't eat their woman's cookie don't get Christmas presents."

"Fuck you," Seth said, shoving his arm away.

"No thanks, but Laura might when she finds out I'm more than willing to lick her—"

"Out of line," I said, my voice cold. "That's fucked up, Adrian."

Adrian opened his mouth to respond, but when he saw the look on my face, raised his hands and turned back to Seth. There was a difference between the usual trash talk we all did and what he'd just said, namely that Seth was clearly pissed off about the whole situation. I mean, he looked like he was about to jump on the shorter man and beat the shit out of him.

Which Adrian would have absolutely deserved. I mean, I could tolerate people talking about how hot Halle was because frankly, she fucking *was*. But if someone sat there and said they were gonna fuck my girlfriend because I wasn't doing it right, I'd... well.

I'd probably lose it.

"Sorry, Seth," Adrian said, and it sounded like he genuinely meant it. "I just mean, like, you're missing out, buddy. There is nothing—and I mean *nothing*—like having a woman writhing underneath you as you just bury your face against her."

"Or sitting on your face," Jay added, likely to help direct the conversation back to a point that didn't have a high risk of manslaughter.

Kendra made a soft *mmm* sound. "Yeah, like when she grinds against your tongue and basically rides your mouth?"

"Exactly," Jay said. "The only reason Candice doesn't *beg* for it is because I like it as much as she does, but she'll still ask for it whenever she wants it."

"And you only have to do it good once before they ask you for it again and again," Adrian said. "Even the one-nighters. And trust me, man. The scent and the taste and the fucking sounds she makes. And how you can barely hear them because her legs just—" He smacked a fist into the open palm of his other hand "—just clamp around your head. And when she's coming and grabbing at your hair like she's trying to pop your head right off your neck?" He made a chef's-kiss gesture. "Fucking glorious."

"Rob wouldn't know about the hair thing," Benny said.

Normally, I'd have some snappy response about being sexier bald than he was with hair—which was true—but I was a bit preoccupied listening to them talk.

Because something had got me thinking, and the hair thing wasn't the only part I didn't really know about.

Halle and I had been together for five years. I was gonna marry her one day. The only reason I hadn't put a ring on it was because she said she wanted us to buy a house first. But I already knew how I was going to propose: it was gonna be the very day we moved into that house, before we'd brought in any of the boxes or furniture or anything. She was my forever, plain and simple, and I knew I was hers.

I loved everything about her: Her tattoos and piercings. Her Rapunzel-like blonde hair. Her laugh. Her beautiful blue eyes. Her heart and how she cared about everyone she came across. The way she could get down and dirty just as easily as she could act prim and proper. And the way she'd just submit to me, let me take control of her body and her pleasure, beg me to wrap my hand around her throat and—

I had to stop that line of thought. I was still at fucking work.

The point was that Halle was the most amazing woman in the world. And of course I thought she was the hottest one, too. I made sure to show her that every time we fucked. Our sex life was good and she always got off, but...

But maybe she didn't like it when I went down on her.

I knew she liked getting oral. She'd told me that at some point, way back when we first started dating. But all that stuff that Adrian and Kendra and Jay were saying...

Halle never sat on my face.

She never... what did Adrian say... *writhed*.

Or clamped her legs around my head.

I mean, frankly, she... she never came when I ate her out.

And that hadn't worried me. She'd said she had a hard time getting off like that, which was fair. She *always* got off when we fucked, even if I'd already finished and had to do it with my hands. I wanted to please her because her pleasure *was* my pleasure. I loved knowing I could make her explode and tremble and clutch at me as the walls of her pussy clenched around my cock or my fingers.

But she never reacted like that when I went down on her.

Actually, I mused as the rest of them kept talking, it wasn't just that. Not only did she not ask me to go down on her or come on my tongue or ride my face, she was usually the one who stopped me. She'd gently urge me away from her pussy, pulling me up to kiss her and plead with me to fuck her. I always thought it was because she was so turned on she couldn't wait any longer, but...

I mean, all the other guys were saying their girls asked for it. And what Adrian had said... when it was good, they'd ask for it again, and...

Oh, fuck.

I was a fucking idiot.

"Earth to Rob?" Adrian said, breaking me out of my thoughts.

"I know it's hot to think about fucking Halle, but you can't go getting all turned on at work," Kendra teased.

I tried to laugh, but nothing came out. And when I didn't tell Kendra to fuck off for talking about Halle like that, Jay frowned at me.

"What's wrong, man?" he asked.

"I think I might be shit at eating pussy," I said.

Chapter Five

Candice

"Do you think I scared Laura off?" I asked.

"I mean, I've never seen someone leave a cookie exchange looking so pale," Trish said as we stepped around a slow-walking grandma.

"She's pale to begin with, though."

"No, she's not," Phoebe piped in quietly from the other side of Trish.

"Well, she's not as pale as *you*," I conceded. "But she was fine, right? It was just one little question about pussy eating."

"I would say it was more than one little question," Trish said. "I think the *little* part of it went out the window when you started describing how deep Jay can get his tongue in your—"

"Merry Christmas, Mrs. Wilson!" I said loudly, waving at the elderly woman I knew from the community league as she walked past us in the opposite direction. She widened her eyes, then looked away quickly.

"I'm just so disappointed in him," I said.

"Who?" Trish asked.

"Seth. I thought he was better than that."

"He might have a good reason for it," Trish said.

"And Laura might just not like it that much," Phoebe said.

"That's total bullshit. Anyone who says they don't enjoy getting their pussy ate is a liar," I said.

Even though Trish sighed and looked at me pointedly, it still took a minute before I realized what I'd said. By then, Phoebe's cheeks were pink and she was chewing on her bottom lip.

"Sorry," I said. "That was harsh. I forgot you don't."

"It's fine," Phoebe said.

"You just need to stop thinking about other people's sex lives," Trish said. "What happens between Seth and Laura is their business. No one else's."

"That is true," I said. "But have you considered that other people's sex lives are interesting?"

"I have considered that," Trish said as Phoebe giggled. "And that makes me wonder just how much you were talking up Jay's skills, since if your *own* sex life was interesting enough, you might not need to focus on others so much."

I cackled, drawing looks from the bustling shoppers around us. But I couldn't help it. People said that whole honeymoon phase where you can't keep your hands off each other faded a few months after getting married, but Jay and I had been married for twelve years and that honeymoon phase hadn't slowed down even once. We made time for sex almost every day and the days that we didn't just felt wrong. No matter how tired my husband was when he got home from work, he wanted to touch me. To kiss me. To squeeze me, hold me, lick me, fuck me... *God*.

"Trish, the worst part about being married to Jay is that I know I'm keeping a literal sex god from the rest of the female population," I said. "Trust me. My husband *knows* his way around the sack. Which is why I think every woman deserves a man that makes her feel as good as Jay makes me feel."

"And you're just a snoop," she said.

"I am a snoop," I agreed, then slowed as I spotted a store I wanted to go into. "And right now, I think I'm gonna snoop for a little extra special Christmas present for Jay."

Trish raised her eyebrows. "From Lacy Pleasures?"

"My sister works there," Phoebe said.

"Does your sister give special discounts on seasonal lingerie to her sister's coworker's sister-in-law?" I asked.

Phoebe shrugged. "Probably. I never use her friends-and-family discount."

"Perfect. I think some Christmas lingerie is in order," I said. "You can both help me pick out something that'll blow Jay's mind."

"I think you just need to strip down naked for that," Trish said.

The cookie exchange had been a blast. I'd been a bit sad when Denise said she wouldn't be able to make it, but Laura had been eager to attend, so the numbers all worked out anyway. And I did quite like Laura. She'd been good for Seth in the months since they'd been together. And they looked so damn cute together. Laura, with her pretty blonde hair and big brown eyes and gorgeous figure. Seth, who looked like he could've been a jock in high school, but the nice guy kind who was probably friends with everyone.

I was rooting for them. I really was.

But she didn't know anyone at the cookie exchange super well, so there was a chance that our informal survey about whether men went down on women for their pleasure or for ours—the results of which I hadn't found overly surprising, but some of the others had—had been a little much for her. I'd have to ask Halle the next time we chatted, since she and Laura lived in the same general direction and had walked home together. Shortly after they left, Nadia had sighed and said she better get home to relieve her husband from her kids, leaving Phoebe and Trish at my place. I wasn't quite ready for the day to end, so I'd suggested the mall for some last minute holiday bargain shopping.

And lingerie shopping, because why not? Jay deserved a little treat.

"Pheebs!" said a tall, slim saleswoman the moment we walked into the lingerie store. She beelined towards us, heels clacking against the tile floor. "Thank God. Finally, something good happens today."

I couldn't help but think she was almost a spitting image of Phoebe, with her thick black hair and pinkish-white skin. She was thinner, yes, but had the same general body shape and fairy-tale princess aura about her. Her lips were painted red and she was wearing an all-black outfit that looked elegant and sexy all at once.

"Everything okay?" Phoebe asked as she approached.

The woman gave her a tired but genuine smile. "Just insanely busy and you are a sight for sore eyes."

Phoebe smiled and hugged the woman, then turned to us. "Olivia, you remember my coworker, Trish? This is her sister-in-law, Candice."

"Nice to meet you," I said, extending my hand.

"And you," Olivia said. "Were you the one doing the cookie exchange today?"

"Yep, that would be me."

Olivia looked down at the bag in my hand and then up at me with a serious, pointed expression. "And you didn't bring any to share with your friendly local lingerie peddler during the Christmas rush? Rude."

I liked her already.

"Tell you what," I said. "I'm looking for something that'll make my husband drop to his knees and bury his face in my—"

"—oh *hi* again, Mrs. Wilson! Merry Christmas!" Trish said abruptly.

Poor Mrs. Wilson looked like she was about to have a heart attack as she turned away from us and headed towards the BBB section—that is, the Basic Beige Bra section.

"... so if you can help me find that, I'll come back with an entire tray of cookies for you," I finished saying to Olivia, who was struggling not to laugh.

"I think I have just the thing."

She motioned for me to follow her, which I did, then stopped when I realized Phoebe was hovering awkwardly near the entrance.

"Are you coming, Phoebe?" I asked.

She looked at me with her wide eyes. "I... you want me to see you try on lingerie?"

I shrugged. "Why not? I need honest opinions and possibly a few sassy jokes, which are your specialty."

She tilted her head to the side thoughtfully, then shrugged and followed me.

Olivia led us to the back of the store, which had a selection of expensive scraps of lace displayed tastefully on mannequins that had no nipples or heads. She asked my size and pulled a few options of lacy scraps from the racks. After picking a few myself and attempting to talk Trish into trying on a leather-and-lace corset-style bustier that she was eyeing, Olivia took us to the private fitting room with a cozy looking couch, soft lighting, and a large mirror.

"Look at us with the VIP treatment," I said, impressed, while she pulled back the curtain to the change area.

"I usually hate VIP duty," Olivia said. "Except for not having to be out on the sales floor while people are trying things on. But you don't seem like you're going to yell at me, so..."

"I might yell at you for costing me too much money if these all look good, but I'll still bring you the cookies."

"Worth it," she said.

The first set I tried on was awful. I burst out laughing and poked my head out of the curtain.

"Do you ladies want to see this?" I asked. "Full disclosure, you *will* see ninety-six percent of my ass cheeks and I don't promise the remaining four percent isn't under something that's completely see-through."

"I want to see it," Trish said, and Phoebe blushed.

I wasn't a small woman.

I'd never *been* a small woman. My body was all hips and boobs and junk in the trunk, with thick and jiggling thighs. And there was a whole society of people who tried to tell me that kind of body was wrong, but as my grandma used to say, "They don't have to live in it, so fuck 'em." I liked my body and its curves. So did my husband, not that his opinion made my body more valid.

But having a bigger body did mean that sometimes, things that should have *theoretically* looked good were... well, awful.

"Oh my God," Trish said when I let the curtain go.

Phoebe had clapped her hand to her mouth, but she let out a relieved giggle when she saw me laughing.

"Oh, no," Olivia said, looking horrified.

I waved a hand at her as I admired myself in the mirror. "Don't worry. This is one of the sets I picked myself. Apparently, I have horrendous taste today."

It was green, which was the first problem; green looked awful on me. There was fur trim along the bottom of the bra, not that anyone could see it. The top part lacked any sort of under wire or support whatsoever, so my tits were hanging over the bottom and covered the embellishment completely. But the main issue was that it was one of those teddy bodysuits, and the designers of the garment seemed to think that the *wider* a body was, the *longer* it also was.

In other words, it was not built for short, fat girls, so the crotch of the teddy was... hanging.

"That's a new designer," Olivia said, cringing. "We just started carrying the larger sizes. But I, uh... don't think we'll be carrying them for much longer."

"It's like they just took something for a straight-sized woman and just stretched it in every direction," Phoebe said, and Olivia looked at her sister apologetically, her cheeks red as she bit her lip.

"I'm assuming the other sets were made for actual plus-sized people," I said.

"Oh, yes. Try that gold lace one on next," Olivia said. "That one is a personal favourite and I think it'll look phenomenal on you."

She was right about that one.

And the next one.

And two more that I couldn't decide between.

"I told you I was going to yell at you if these cost me too much money," I scolded as I admired the final lingerie set in the mirror. This one was green, too, but it was a much nicer green done in material that looked like crushed velvet, paired with black leather trim that was so soft, I didn't want to stop running my hands over it.

Olivia glanced at Phoebe. "Well, *maybe* if my little sister also found something sexy today, I could swing a little friends-and-family discount your way."

CHAPTER SIX
Candice

"No," Phoebe said immediately. "I don't need any lingerie."

Trish's face lit up. "Oh, come on, Pheebs! Miguel would love that."

Phoebe shook her head. "I don't do the lingerie thing. It's just not me."

"Have you ever worn it?" I asked.

She pressed her lips together, then sighed. "Well, no, but—"

"Then how do you know you don't like it?" Trish asked.

"I... I just do," Phoebe said, her voice softer than usual. "I don't like lingerie. It... it gets in the way."

There was something to that softness that wasn't quite truthful. I stopped touching the leather and velvet on the lingerie set and turned towards her.

"You would look *so* good in that red babydoll Candice tried on," Trish said. "The one with the high-waisted thong that laced up in the back?"

"I wouldn't," Phoebe said.

"You totally would," Trish argued. "I would wear that in a heartbeat."

For all her quietness and dry wit, I'd never seen Phoebe get upset. But just then, pink patches appeared on her cheeks and she glared up at Trish, her jaw trembling.

"And you have no idea what it's like to be a bigger girl," she snapped. "Do you know how uncomfortable I'd feel in that? How *awful* my body would look in it?"

33

Silence filled the small VIP area. Phoebe's face went even redder and Olivia bit her lip again, a look of heartbreak in her eyes. I looked from her to Phoebe, then down at my lingerie.

"Did you think it looked awful on my body, Pheebs?" I asked.

Phoebe whipped her head towards me, her eyes wide. "What? No, of course—"

"Because you and I have pretty similar body types," I said. "And I looked like a fucking goddess in that set."

She opened her mouth, then closed it. "It's not... not the same. All of these look amazing on you because you don't have a belly like I do. You're not shaped like I am."

"She kind of is, though," Olivia said gently. "I know you're insecure about your stomach, Pheebs, but that's in your head. If you thought it looked good on Candice, it's going to look good on you, too."

"Trish might not know what it's like to be plus-size, but I do," I said bluntly. "And I promise you, Pheebs, you're going to feel like a queen in it."

She looked like she was about to cry. "I just don't think I'll look good in it the way you do."

"Well, I *know* you would." I picked up the set off the rack and held it out to her. "Here. Just try it and we'll stop bothering you. Just one."

She stared at the lingerie hanging on the hanger, then hesitantly reached out and took it. When she didn't move towards the changing room, I raised my eyebrows and gestured towards it.

"Aren't you going to change first?" she asked me.

"Why? Look how cute I am in this," I said. "They'll be lucky to get it off me so they can scan it at the till."

"We could just take the tags off and scan those," Olivia said helpfully.

I smiled. "See? Go try it on. I'm going to sit on that couch and *lounge* in my lingerie."

She licked her lips, then nodded before looking at me with a pained expression. "I'm sorry I said, um... or, well, implied that—"

"You don't need to be sorry," I said. "I get it, Pheebs. I've been there. But being in a smaller body isn't necessary for happiness. You're allowed to be happy how you are, especially when you're a fucking bombshell like you and I are."

She laughed. It was a watery, shaky sound that I felt deep in my heart, but it was a laugh all the same.

"Now go change," I said to her. "I'm ready for the fashion show."

I wasn't upset in the slightest about what Phoebe had said. I knew all too well how she was feeling and just how damn hard it was to escape from those thoughts. But they were completely unjustified. Phoebe was incredibly beautiful. That black hair and big eyes and her *curves*? The way she wore the hell out of that sweater dress that looked like it had been tailor-made for her?

I had no idea why she was self-conscious about her tummy. I couldn't honestly say I'd ever noticed it on her before, but I knew how little that mattered. *She* noticed it, and that made it a hard thing to overcome.

But she would. Because I knew I wasn't the only person who thought she was gorgeous. And as she walked out of the change room a few minutes later, I thought there might be one more person in the world who thought so, too.

"Oh my gosh," Olivia said in a hushed voice that sounded eerily like her sister's.

"Wow," Trish said.

"Told you so," I added.

Phoebe laughed, but she didn't argue. There was a hint of red in her eyes and I had a feeling she'd had a bit of a cry in the change room while she got dressed, but if she had, the tears were long gone. She was wearing that red babydoll like she'd been born to do it. Approaching the mirror, she brushed her long, black hair over one shoulder and studied her reflection for a moment.

"It does look nicer than I thought it would," she admitted.

"*Nice*?!" I said. "Girl, that is the *last* word I would use to describe this. Miguel is about to find out what happens when his sexy fucking girlfriend makes it onto Santa's naughty list."

Her face went beet red, but she laughed as she admired herself in the mirror. "You think he'll like it?"

"He's going to rip it to shreds," Trish said. "Take some photos of yourself before showing it to him because I'm willing to bet it'll last about thirty seconds before he gives into his primal urges."

I snorted. "'Primal urges'?"

"You know I'm right."

"Yeah, but you don't have to *call* it that."

Phoebe pursed her lips. "So you think I should get it?"

"Pheebs, let me tell you this from the bottom of my heart," Olivia said before either Trish or I could knock some sense into Phoebe. "If you don't buy that today, I'm going to buy it for you. And then I'm going to wrap it up and put it under the Christmas tree and you're going to unsuspectingly open it in front of Mom and Dad at Christmas dinner next week."

"You wouldn't!" Phoebe said.

"I would. So if you want to give Miguel a fighting chance at *not* giving in to his 'primal urges' in front of our parents—"

"You're the worst sister," Phoebe muttered. "Fine. But I want a good discount if you think he's going to shred it anyway."

Olivia practically beamed. "Maybe you should get a second set, just in case."

She didn't quite talk Phoebe into another set of lingerie, but that was okay. One was a start, and even though Phoebe's face was the same colour as the discreet blush pink bags we walked out of Lacy Pleasures with after changing, I felt like we'd made some progress with her that day.

And I was about to make more.

"Phoebe, is the reason you weren't into lingerie before the same as why you don't like getting your pussy eaten?" I asked as we walked towards the exit of the mall.

"Candice!" Trish squeaked. "Rude."

But if Phoebe thought it was, she didn't say so. Instead, she glanced down at the ground, her shoulders hunching forward a bit.

"It is, isn't it?" I asked, though I tried to make my voice a bit gentler.

"It's hard," she admitted. "I mean, I try not to let it get to me and be confident or whatever, but I just... I freeze up. It's hard enough to be naked with someone, let alone have him... you know. Right *there*."

I put an arm around her shoulders. "I know. I mean, I really know."

She sighed. "But you're so confident."

"I am now. I wasn't always. But you know what?"

"What?"

"You're hot, Pheebs."

Her face turned red and she giggled.

"You are," I insisted. "You're gorgeous. And Miguel thinks so, too. I mean, obviously. So you know what you do?"

"What?"

"You go home, put your new sexy set on, and show him the woman he sees every time he looks at you. Then you grab a towel, walk up to him, and wipe his face."

Trish looked as bewildered as Phoebe did. "Why?"

I blinked at them both innocently. "Well, when he asks that, you say you're just cleaning your seat before you sit down."

Phoebe clapped a hand to her mouth to stifle her laughter. "I can't. I can't do that."

"What? Wipe his face or sit on it?"

"Sit on it," she said, her voice so quiet it was almost non-existent. "What if I crush him?"

I stopped walking and turned to her, an unimpressed look on my face as I folded my arms.

"Girl, let me tell you something," I said. "First of all, if it's too much for him, he'll try to get you to move. He's still got arms and the ability to use them. Second of all, if for some reason he *doesn't*, you'll figure out he's not breathing when he stops moving and you're like, 'what the fuck, why did you stop eating my pussy?'"

She stared at me, her eyes wide.

"But here's the thing," I continued. "I can tell you I've sat on Jay's face multiple times a week for the past fifteen or so years and I've yet to kill him. Suffocate him enough to cause some brain damage? Maybe. But that's a *him* problem for not telling me to move soon enough."

"You think?" she asked.

I nodded. "Just try it, Pheebs. Like, at least you've got a guy who's willing to do it. Can you imagine being Laura and Seth not being willing to even try?"

"So sad," Trish murmured, and Phoebe let out a giggle.

I don't know that I actually convinced her to sit on Miguel's face, but she was at least smiling as we left the mall.

The rest of the day passed slowly. After Phoebe and Trish went to their respective homes, I went back to my place and cleaned up the rest of the mess from the cookie exchange, then took a shower and changed into one of the new lingerie sets I'd bought—a very festive lacy set that had crotchless panties and snowflake-shaped buttons down the front. Then, I got into bed, grabbed a book, and waited.

When he texted me a little while later, I grinned, expecting it to say he was on his way.

But it didn't.

I'm going to grab a drink with the guys before heading home, it said. *Go ahead and order something for dinner without me and I'll see you in a couple hours.*

Instead of typing a message, I pointed my camera down my body and snapped a quick photo, sending it without comment. Moments later, my phone went off again.

I'll be home in 15.

CHAPTER SEVEN

Benny

"To Benny's old lady, who is way cooler than Jay's old lady, and let him go out for drinks after work," Adrian said, raising his pint of beer.

I folded my arms. "My *wife's* name is Denise. Don't call her my '*old lady*.'"

Adrian rolled his eyes. "It's just an expression. Right, Rob?"

The tall, bald man beside him jerked his head up. "Huh?"

"Oh, here we go again," Adrian said, sighing. "Dude, you have to stop moping."

"I'm not moping," Rob grumbled as he moped into his beer. "I'm just thinking."

Adrian and I exchanged a look.

Rob had been "just thinking" all day, ever since Jay had gotten that little question from his wife. It was kind of alarming to watch, honestly. If Southbush had a biker bar, that's probably where we would've gone instead of Whiskey Sours, since Rob could've intimidated even the meanest motherfucker there with his towering height and countless tattoos. For some people, moping around the job site all afternoon would have been closer to the pathetic side of things than the worrying side of things, but for a guy with Rob's stature, it was just *scary*. I mean, I was an average-size dude and Rob was a good eight or nine inches taller than me.

That's not the kind of guy you want to rub the wrong way, you know?

It had been alarming enough that just before quitting time rolled around, Adrian pulled me to the side and asked if I was busy that night, since Rob seemed like he needed some cheering up. And as it happened, I wasn't—Denise had taken our two sons to her mom's for a visit and said she was staying for dinner—so I agreed to it.

"Who's up for a pint before heading home?" Adrian announced. "Rob? You're in."

Rob shook his head. "No, I'm—"

"—coming along and that's final." Adrian turned to Jay. "Boss-man?"

"Not your boss," Jay grumbled. "But sure, I'll come."

Adrian pointed finger guns at Seth. "Seth, baby?"

But Seth shook his head, and even when Adrian tried pulling the same thing as he had with Rob, still insisted he wasn't coming. Adrian had looked to me for support, but I shook my head subtly.

I mean, I was half-surprised the kid had made it until the end of the day. After that little question of Candice's, he looked like he wanted the ground to eat him whole. Or to lose his shit on someone for implying he wasn't pleasing his girlfriend. Especially Adrian, who had definitely gone a bit too far with the teasing.

Kendra bowed out too, citing her pregnant wife having a craving for a specific chicken sandwich from a fast-food place that was only available in the next town over, which I could definitely commiserate on. Then, as we were walking to our trucks, Jay had looked at his phone and casually said he had to get home and would take us up on the offer another day.

Adrian had made fun of him, but I'd caught a glimpse of the screen before Jay had hurriedly tilted it away, and while I couldn't say I'd seen any details on the photo, I saw enough to know he was making the right choice.

But that left just me and Adrian taking Rob out for a drink to cheer him up. And so far, Rob had been resistant to our attempts.

"Rob," I said as kindly as I could. "You're in your head about this. Halle didn't say shit about you being bad in bed. *You* came to that conclusion based on a bunch of other people's opinions."

Rob glared at me. "Of course I did. When you're sitting there listening to everyone else talk about how their girls beg for it and the only ones that don't are the ones who apparently don't like it, what else are you supposed to think?" He lifted his beer but paused before sipping it. "And I didn't fucking say I was bad in bed. Just at... at..."

"Eating pussy," Adrian finished. "I mean, granted, it *is* a learned skill. But not a hard one to master. If Benny can do it well enough that his old lady—"

"Call her that one more time and I'll crack a pool cue over your head," I said. "And I just said it doesn't do that much for me. Like, the act itself. It's kind of a turn on because... you know. Pussy. Face. Sex is about to happen. Like I mean, what about blowjobs?"

"I am in support of blowjobs," Adrian said.

I rolled my eyes. "I just mean for people giving blowjobs, sucking someone's dick probably doesn't turn on the suck-er as much as the suck-ee."

"There are plenty of suck-ers that get turned on by giving blowjobs," Adrian replied.

"But arguably, it's about the suck-ee's pleasure more than anything," I said.

"Can we just stop talking about oral sex?" Rob said, sighing.

"Nah," Adrian said. "We're going to figure out if you suck at it."

Rob looked up, bewildered. "What?"

"Talk us through it," Adrian said. "Look, not to brag, but I've had women beg me for my number after a one-night stand so I can go down on them again."

"You're so full of shit," I said.

Adrian took a sip of beer, looking at me smugly. "Believe what you want, wife guy. I know where my talents lie."

"Yeah. As an excellent storyteller."

That got a chuckle out of Rob. Adrian tilted his glass towards him.

"Storyteller or not, I can help you figure this out. And Benny can sit here and be useless like always," Adrian said.

"Useful enough that someone decided I was worth marrying," I said. "How many serious relationships have you had, man-whore?"

"In this situation, my man-whoreness is much more useful," Adrian argued. "We're not trying to figure out if Rob is husband material. We're trying to figure out if he sucks at eating pussy."

From beside us, the server—a nice girl named Gwen who always chatted with Denise whenever we came here for dinner—cleared her throat, her face red. "Um, does anyone want to order food?"

"Nachos?" I asked the other two.

"You don't want a bucket of clams?" Rob said.

Adrian choked on his beer and Gwen swallowed nervously. "We, um, don't serve clams here."

Rob shook his head. "No, I mean... never mind. Nachos is good."

"Guac on the side?"

"Two orders," I said, then handed her the menus and tried to smile apologetically.

Adrian mopped the beer he'd choked on off his face, waiting until the server walked away before speaking again.

"Come on, Robbie," he said. "Let's get you out of this funk. I bet you're perfectly fine at it and you're just overthinking right now."

Rob sighed. "What am I even supposed to tell you?"

"Your technique," Adrian said. "How'd you learn to do it, what you do, how she reacts... just give us all of it."

Rob opened his mouth, then hesitated and closed it. He looked down at his beer, lifted his head, and opened his mouth again... then didn't say anything.

"Do you not have a technique?" Adrian asked.

"What do you even mean by 'technique'?" Rob asked.

Adrian glanced at me before looking back at Rob. "Well, like, I focus a lot on the, uh... *outlying* areas before I get down to business. Really rile them up before even getting to the good part, you know?"

Rob stared at him.

"The clit?" Adrian said, his voice vaguely concerned. "You know where that—"

"Of course I fucking know where that is!" Rob snapped.

"Okay, so what do you *do* to it?" I asked. "Do you suck on it? Rub your tongue on it? Lick? Flick? Circle?"

He turned to me, the anger on his face fading just enough that I could see it was masking a worried look of confusion. "I... I mean... I dunno. I mostly, like, put my tongue... in? And then I do the alphabet thing."

Adrian and I didn't even look at each other before reacting. He slapped the table and I leaned back in my chair, wincing.

"Oh, *no*," I groaned.

"Not the alphabet thing," Adrian said.

"What?" Rob asked defensively. "What's wrong with the alphabet thing?"

"Oh, poor Halle," Adrian said. "Dude, just... just no. The alphabet thing doesn't work."

"It's a total urban legend," I agreed. "Just... just don't do that, man."

"What's wrong with it?" he asked, his face turning red.

I exchanged a look with Adrian, who was still grimacing. He shook his head, then grabbed his beer, chugged the remaining half of it, and put the glass down on the table loudly enough that the server looked over so he could raise his hand and order another pint.

"Who told you to do that?" Adrian asked.

"I don't know," Rob muttered. "I just, like, heard that. As a teenager or something. And I mean, I watch porn, you assholes."

"Teenagers are fucking morons and porn isn't real." Adrian sat up straight. "Okay. Throw out everything you know about eating pussy. We're starting from scratch."

Chapter Eight

Benny

"So you're saying I do suck at it," Rob said.

"Dude, you just told us you use your tongue like a mouth penis and ignore any sense of consistency by spelling out twenty-six individual letters on your girl's clit," Adrian said. "Yeah, you suck."

"I can ask Gwen for some paper and a pen if you want to take notes," I said.

Rob's glare was so strong I almost felt it, but it was worth the laugh.

"Okay, lesson one," Adrian said, pinching the bridge of his nose before scooting his chair closer to the table. "The clit is the little nub that's right at the top of—"

"I know where her fucking clit is!" Rob said.

"I said throw out everything you know about eating pussy."

"Eating pussy isn't the only reason to know where the clit is," I said.

"He thought the alphabet thing was an acceptable pussy-eating technique, Benny," Adrian said. "Can we trust that he actually knows where it is?"

I tilted my head. "Good point. Okay, so Rob, the clit is kind of at the top of the—"

"Fuck you both," Rob muttered.

He stopped sulking enough to let Adrian share some tips with him, and honestly, once we got past making sure Rob knew where the clit was—which, to his credit, he did—I was pretty useless. As much as I hated to admit it, Adrian really *did* seem to know what he was talking about, and I was more than happy to let him talk.

I mean, it felt kind of weird to be the guy who knew what he was doing, at least more than Rob did. I was secure enough in myself to be able to admit that both Rob and Adrian were attractive dudes. Slightly terrifying, in Rob's case, but the muscles and broad shoulders and shaved head look was a good one for him. And Adrian was good-looking, too. He was half-Indian and had thick, glossy black hair and a classically handsome face. At the moment, he was dressed in his coveralls and work boots, but he was also one of those stylish guys who knew how to dress himself well and owned like... I dunno. Wool peacoats and shit.

Then there was me: the dad-bod ginger with pasty white skin and shaggy red hair. Sure, I worked the same job these guys did, but I never built muscle the same way they managed to.

Probably because they went to the gym and stuff.

But I didn't have time for that kind of thing. I got my cardio in by chasing a seven-year-old and my weight training by hefting a chunky four-year-old up on my shoulders regularly. My wardrobe consisted mostly of free beer t-shirts and that one hoodie I'd had since at least before my first kid was born. And whatever pair of jeans had the least amount of holes in it until Denise forced me to go shopping, where I'd buy five identical pairs of jeans and call it a day.

But that was okay. My wife liked me well enough, and I was happy with our life. Being a dad was what I was meant to do; I'd realized that the second Denise got pregnant the first time. My family was everything to me and that was how I liked it. I had my kids, my gorgeous wife, a good job, a great sex life... I was the richest man in the world.

Although, I did pick up a few new tips on the sex front that night.

"Don't take her panties off," Adrian said at one point. "Kiss everything through the fabric. I know this sounds like the least sexy thing in the world, but like, use your lips to kind of 'squeeze' hers through her panties."

"With her panties on?" Rob repeated. "Does that actually feel good?"

Adrian looked annoyed. "When you grab your cock through your boxers, does it feel good?"

"I mean, yeah, but not as good as—"

"You're building up tension," Adrian said. "You'll get under the panties eventually. Just trust the process, man."

"And what if she's not wearing panties?"

"Then do it without the panties!" Adrian threw his hands up in the air. "Just use some common sense. Improvise. *Adapt.*"

Rob nodded, his face red all the way up to where his hairline would have been, if he had hair.

"Hickeys," Adrian said a few minutes later, and I raised my eyebrows in surprise.

"Really?" I asked.

Adrian nodded. "Inner thighs. Trust me. Don't be too rough because the skin there is *sensitive*, but leaving a few little hickeys around there is so fucking hot."

"For her or for me?" Rob asked dryly.

"Mostly for you, but sucking on those spots feels good for her too," Adrian said. "Now, by my understanding, you learned all your sex techniques from teenage boys, so you should know how to leave a hickey, but—"

Rob threw a nacho at him, which Adrian caught with a laugh.

He kept giving Rob tips, talking him through what he said was a patented technique, even though I was pretty sure you couldn't patent a pussy-eating technique. What was more, though, was just the *passion* he spoke with about it.

My wife loved oral. Given the choice, Denise probably would've picked that over actual intercourse every single time. Not that she did, because obviously we had... well, currently had two kids, but I'd known from before we even got married that getting eaten out was her *thing*.

For me, it was... okay. I liked that she liked it. I'm sure Denise wished my heart was in it a little more, but I couldn't change how I felt. She knew what she wanted and had spelled out what I needed to do while I was down there, and I did that dutifully every time. It just got a little... well, boring. Repetitive.

But it made her come, and that was what mattered. But listening to the way Adrian talked about it...

There was no way I'd ever fucking admit it, but the way he was describing eating pussy was seriously turning me on.

"... so at that point, she should be squirming," Adrian said, his voice low, and at some point we had all leaned in over the table to talk in hushed voices. "That's when you know. If she hasn't already taken her panties off, that's when you do it."

I twisted my mouth to the side. Denise always relaxed back against the bed. She'd run her hand through my hair, but the only *squirming* she did was when she was coming and tightened her thighs around my neck. If I could make her squirm with anticipation...

"Do I keep teasing her after I take her panties off?" Rob whispered.

"You can, but I don't usually bother doing much of that," Adrian replied. "Like, her panties should be completely soaked by that point, so she's more than ready for the next step."

"Which is...?"

A coy smile spread across Adrian's face. "The vortex."

Both Rob and I blinked at him.

"The fuck is the vortex?" I finally asked.

"There are a few different versions," Adrian said. "You make your mouth into an 'O' shape, okay? Then put it over her clit and—"

I'd already started shaking my head. "That doesn't work for everyone."

Adrian raised his eyebrows. "Are you arguing with the pussy-eating master?"

"I'm saying my wife doesn't enjoy having her clit sucked. She specifically told me that."

"She probably didn't have it done right," Adrian argued. "Do you suck at eating pussy, too?"

"Fuck you," I said. "She comes every time I do it. But she's told me what she likes, and that was something she said didn't feel good."

Adrian shrugged. "It's possible, but in my experience, women say that when they've had bad experiences. You don't suck hard. And it's not like when you get your dick sucked. Clits are *way* more sensitive than dicks are. So the vortex is more about pressure than anything. You're surrounding the clit with your lips almost... I dunno. Like, 'pulsing' is a better word than 'sucking.'"

"It sounds like sucking," I said.

He shook his head. "Trust me, man. Get Denise to let you try it, and if you're doing it right, she'll be a puddle underneath you in seconds."

I hummed, lifting my beer to my mouth. "I dunno. She likes the flat tongue technique."

"What's that?" Rob asked.

We were past making fun of him for having the sexual knowledge of a teenager with a shoddy internet connection.

"You flatten your tongue like—" I stopped and glanced around, making sure no one was paying attention to us. "—like this." I stuck my tongue out and flattened it, showing him what I meant.

"So you just lick with a really wide tongue," Rob said.

I shook my head. "You're not moving your tongue. Move your head. Start from the bottom and like..." I glanced around again, then tried to do the motion, though I kept my tongue in my mouth.

"It is a good technique, despite the fact that Benny looks like a ginger chicken right now," Adrian said, and I rolled my eyes.

"And then what?" Rob asked.

"Then... keep doing it?" I said.

"That's it? Just... that?"

"I mean, consistency is key," Adrian said. "You can change things up a bit. Like if you're doing the vortex, you can kind of get your tongue involved or change up the pressure, but you should do it sort of... you know. In the same pattern?"

"Rhythmically," I said.

Adrian nodded. "Yeah. Women like consistency. I mean, the golden rule here is that whatever you're doing, if she's into it, *keep fucking doing it.*"

Rob's throat flexed as he swallowed. "And how do I know if she's into it?"

"Her reactions should tell you," I said.

"And if she's not reacting?"

I shrugged. "Either she's not into what you're doing, or she legitimately doesn't like oral sex."

He sighed, leaning back in his chair. "So basically, try the vortex and if that doesn't work, try the flat tongue thing, and if *that* doesn't work, just give up."

"You're so fucking dramatic," Adrian said. "No. Get your fingers in there. Get your tongue down at her opening and play around there a little. Or try—"

"Wait," Rob said. "You told me not to use my tongue as a mouth penis."

"Um," said Gwen, who had appeared out of nowhere again. "Does anyone want a refill?"

"I think we scared her," I said after she stumbled away with our drink orders.

"Or she's about to go home and tell her boyfriend to get his head out of his ass and eat her pussy properly," Adrian said. "Either way, not the point. Rob, you don't *fuck* her with your tongue. But you can put it in a bit. It's part of the teasing thing. Everything down there is sensitive, just at different levels. Your focus should be her clit, but everything else helps add to the sensation."

"Right," he said. "Okay."

"Now, what was I saying," Adrian muttered. "Oh yeah. Does Halle like it in the ass?"

I almost jumped out of my chair to hold Rob back, but Adrian lifted his hands.

"It's purely for educational purposes!" he said.

"What the actual *fuck*, man?" Rob growled.

"I'm saying if she's a 'don't touch my asshole ever' kind of person, I'm not going to get into the next level of stuff. But if she's into it..." Adrian looked at me for support, but I shook my head.

"I'm not talking about my wife's asshole with you."

"So Denise doesn't like backdoor stuff," Adrian said confidently. "That's okay. But if Halle does..."

Rob's face was red. He looked at me, then back at Adrian.

"If you ever repeat any of this to her, I will tear your balls off," Rob said.

Adrian mimed zipping his lips shut. "I'm just out here helping a friend, man. I like my balls right where they are."

I didn't pay much attention to what Adrian said after that. He wasn't wrong. Denise was absolutely against any and all things anal-related. And honestly, I didn't mind. Like, I'm sure it felt good or whatever, but given how exquisite my wife's pussy was, I couldn't see how it would feel any *better*. So while they talked about ass stuff that had no relevance to me, I texted Denise to see if she was home with the kids yet.

I'm home, came her response. *Grandma decided the boys should have an impromptu sleepover, so I left them there.*

Perfect.

I put my phone back in my pocket and stood up. "I'm going home."

"What?" Adrian said. "Already? Why?"

"Gonna go attempt the vortex on my wife's clit." I threw some cash on the table, far more than necessary to cover my share. "Have a good one, boys."

Adrian's laughter made heads turn, but I didn't pay any attention to it as I walked out of Whiskey Sours.

CHAPTER NINE

Benny

WHEN I GOT HOME fifteen minutes later, golden lights were spilling out of the windows and I could see the Christmas tree twinkling in the living room. Denise had turned the outside Christmas lights on, too, and they splashed my truck with streaks of red and gold and blue and green as I parked in the driveway. Inside, the heat was on nice and high and I could hear the shower running from the master bedroom.

I licked my lips, kicked my work boots off, and hurried across the house.

"Hey, babe," I called when I got to the bedroom so I didn't startle her.

"Hi!" she replied, her voice echoing in the bathroom.

I undressed quickly, chucking my work clothes in the general direction of the laundry basket with the full intention of cleaning them up after I'd thoroughly ravished my wife. Then I walked to the bathroom and pushed the door open.

The glass door of the shower was mostly steamed up, but I could see the outline of her body on the other side of the fog. Denise had always been petite; she was short and slim, with warm beige-white skin dotted with freckles and short pixie-length hair that she loved to dye a multitude of colours. Right now, it was her natural auburn, since she wouldn't be able to get it done for a while.

Her breasts were already starting to swell, which I loved. I mean, I was absolutely a fan of women on the itty-bitty-titty-committee too, but as soon as Denise started putting a little weight on, it went straight to her boobs, and I wasn't gonna complain about that. And her belly was just starting to show, enough that she'd bowed out of going to the cookie exchange. Between the copious amounts of alcohol and the inability to cover the swell of her stomach when she wasn't wearing loose, flowing dresses, the other women would have figured it out instantly and Denise wasn't quite ready to tell everyone we were expecting our third.

"It's our last one," she had said after our first doctor's appointment. "I just want to keep it to ourselves for a while."

Which had been hell, because all I wanted to do was scream out into the night that my wife was pregnant again and I was going to be a dad for the third time, but there would be time for that later. This was what Denise wanted, and I wanted to give her everything she wanted. She'd started showing a lot earlier than with our two boys, which she complained about because it made things a bit more difficult to hide. But besides my suspicions that it meant we were having a girl this time, I didn't mind.

She was *so* fucking hot when she was pregnant.

"Is there room for me in there?" I asked.

She turned her head, sticking her tongue out at me from the other side of the glass door. "I'm not *that* big yet, you jerk."

I grinned. "Not what I meant and you know it, pipsqueak."

A flood of steam poured out of the shower when I opened the door. At the same time, Denise shivered, goosebumps raising along her arms as I let out some of the heat. I stepped in quickly, pulling the door shut behind me as the spray of water that was *way* too fucking hot hit me.

"You got dirty today," she said as dark dust began to run off me before I'd even grabbed the soap.

"We worked hard," I replied.

"But you'll finish by tomorrow like Dave said?"

I nodded, grabbing the bottle of body wash. "Might even finish a little early. We'll see. But it's just about done."

"Good." She took the bottle from my hands and flicked the cap open, then tilted it upside down in her hand and squirted a healthy amount of the gel into her palm. "Come here. Let me wash you."

"Mmm," I said. "Babe. You don't have to."

She rubbed her hands together, creating a thick lather as she blinked up at me. "I want to."

"I came in here because I wanted to spoil you," I said, but couldn't bring myself to stop her from running her soapy hands along my chest.

"Spoil me?" she repeated. "You already spoil me."

"I mean *really* spoil you."

Her head tilted to the side. "How so?"

I licked my lips, then reached out so I could put my hands on her hips. My cock was already hard because of course it was, because I'd been talking and thinking about pussy all fucking day and now my pregnant wife was wet and naked in front of me. It bumped against the swell of her belly as I pulled her in close.

"I wanna eat your pussy, babe."

Denise's eyebrows raised so high on her forehead that water poured into her eyes. She blinked hard, shaking the drops away before looking back at me.

"You're *asking* to?" she said.

"Yes."

"What... what brought this on?"

I shrugged, then smirked at her. "Call it a pregnancy craving."

She burst out laughing, then let her hands trail down my stomach—which had a belly of its own, but she didn't seem to mind all that much—and down to my pelvis. I let out a soft grunt as her tiny fingers circled around my cock, her hands slippery from the soap and the water, and stroked me gently.

"I know how serious those cravings can get," she said. "Far be it from me to deny you."

I tilted my head down, capturing her lips as water sprayed over us.

"Good," I murmured. "You still okay to lie on your back?"

"I'm not *that* pregnant yet," she said. "Jeez. You'd think we haven't done this twice already."

I hugged her closer, indulging in her naked body and sighing as she handled my cock. "Just making sure, pipsqueak."

We finished washing off as quickly as we could, though it took longer than usual given that I couldn't stop myself from kissing her over and over again. As soon as I felt like the layer of grime from the site was gone, I turned off the tap, still kissing and caressing her as I pulled her out of the shower and towelled her off before drying myself.

I wasn't quite confident enough in my strength to sweep her off her feet, and I wouldn't have risked it anyway given that there was a baby in there and I'd never forgive myself for dropping her, so I used my body to urge her towards the bed.

"I wanna do things a little different this time," I said as we reached it.

Denise raised her eyebrows. "Different?"

I nodded, suddenly nervous. "I wanna, uh, try some different things. Stuff I don't usually do."

"Colour me intrigued," she said, giggling.

"I'll stop if you don't like what I'm doing." I guided her back on the bed, grabbing a pillow and fluffing it so she had somewhere to rest her head, but before she could scoot back, I stopped her. "Keep your ass on the edge of the mattress."

"My butthole is off limits," she warned.

"I know that, pipsqueak. I won't touch it." Leaning over, I kissed her and brushed the auburn hair off her forehead. "Relax and let me take care of you."

"You always take care of me," she whispered, and I couldn't help but smile against her lips.

I started off the same way I usually did when she asked me to go down on her: by going down. I kissed my way from her lips to her chin, her chin down her neck, and her neck to her breasts. Those deserved a little attention on their own, partly because Denise had sensitive little nipples and mostly because boobs.

Like, come on. Boobs are always fantastic and I only had so long to enjoy hers before she had to go and use them for their intended purpose, so I was going to indulge in them as much as I could.

Her nipples hardened beneath my tongue, pebbling into tight little nubs that I flicked my tongue across. She moaned as I did, one hand fluttering to my head and brushing my still-wet hair through her fingers. I shivered as she scratched my scalp, then opened my mouth and took as much of her breast inside it as I could.

I didn't know why, but that always drove her crazy. Especially now, when her boobs were almost too big to actually *fit* in my mouth.

"Fuck, I love it when you do that," she gasped.

I couldn't say anything in response on account of the fact that her entire tit was in my mouth, but I made a soft humming noise and released it just enough that I could focus on her nipple again. She sighed, a content sound, and when I glanced up, her head was tilted back on the pillow.

I figured that meant it was the perfect time for a practice round of one of the new things I wanted to try. You know, just to get the... the *technique* down before trying it on her pussy.

Giving the hardened little nub a final lick, I made the "O" shape with my lips that Adrian had recommended, then took her nipple back in my mouth. Sucking softly, I attempted the pulsing sort of sucking that he'd recommended, flicking my tongue across the very tip of her nipple as I did.

"Oh," Denise said, breathless curiosity in her voice.

I figured that was good, so I did it again. Beneath me, her hips shifted slightly. I didn't know if that counted as a squirm, but it was *something*. Trying not to grin, I cupped her other breast and squeezed before switching my mouth to that side and repeating the action.

"That feels nice," she said.

Fuck, if Adrian was right about the vortex, I was gonna be pissed. Mostly because I'd feel like I'd need to buy him a beer.

After lavishing a good amount of attention on each of her breasts, I half-reluctantly and half-eagerly pulled my mouth away and kept kissing my way down her body. The underside of her tits, her ribs, and a few moments to nuzzle indulgently against her already firm belly. It wasn't big enough for her to feel uncomfortable yet, but I knew it wouldn't be long before it was. And her being uncomfortable was not my favourite part of her being pregnant, obviously, but I'd learned to combat that with some wise tips from my dad, of all people, with our first boy.

"Stand behind her," he'd said at a family dinner while Denise was in our kitchen chatting with my mom, "and put your hands under her belly. Then just lift—*gently* lift—and hold the weight for a bit. If she's not melting back against you with relief, you're doing it wrong."

I hadn't done it wrong. I'd gone into the kitchen a short while later to bring a stack of dirty dishes to the counter and Denise was resting against the sink, grimacing as she held her back. So I did exactly as my dad had said: slipped my hands beneath her stomach, then lifted.

She moaned, then immediately clapped her hand over her mouth.

"It's okay," I whispered in her ear. "Just relax and let me take care of you."

"You're going to be such a good daddy," she murmured as she leaned back against me.

And like, I'd kinda already started *reacting* when she moaned like that, but feeling her body rest against mine paired with that fucking *word*...

"You like being called Daddy?" Denise whispered.

"I don't know if I like it right this second," I breathed back. "Considering my parents are in the next room."

"But later?"

"... maybe," I said in a way that clearly meant yes.

I couldn't see her face, but I could hear the fucking mischievous smile that spread across her lips. "Okay, Daddy."

That had stuck. The word, I mean. After that first pregnancy and the second one and even now, she would whisper that word to me. She knew exactly how to use it to get what she wanted, which she did yet again as I kissed her belly and caressed it with my hands on my way down to eat her pussy.

"Are you just going to keep teasing me, Daddy?" Denise murmured.

I shivered, which made her giggle, and planted a final kiss just below her belly button before I had to shift to kneeling on the soft rug covering the hardwood floor beside our bed.

Her pussy was already getting wet. Not completely, not enough that she was soaking the bedspread beneath her or that it was coating her thighs or anything, but enough that I could see it glistening between her folds. She wasn't wearing panties, so I couldn't exactly tease her through them, but as Adrian had said: Improvise.

Adapt.

CHAPTER TEN

Benny

I KISSED THE TOP of her mound, rubbing my nose in the trimmed triangle of hair, then stuck out my tongue and licked along her pussy lips. Denise sighed and her legs widened a bit, but instead of diving in like I usually would, I turned my head and placed tiny kisses along her groin.

"Mmm," she said from above me. "So you *are* teasing me?"

I glanced up, meeting her eye over the swell of her belly. "You're assuming I'm doing this for you."

Denise's eyes widened in surprise. I tried not to grin, which meant something more like a smirk crossed my face, then focused back on the task at hand.

Or, well. At mouth, I guess.

The little kisses moved from her groin to her inner thigh. I sighed against the silky skin there, parting my lips so I could place open-mouth kisses on the skin Adrian had said was so sensitive. The fucker was right about that too, apparently, because Denise's hips shifted as I picked a spot and sucked on it.

Then they shifted again as I sucked a little harder.

Then she gasped and wiggled so she could prop herself up high enough to watch me.

"You're gonna leave a mark," she said.

"So?"

I glanced up and caught her eye again. Her cheeks were pink and she bit her lip, then released it.

"So... maybe you need to leave a matching one on the other side, Daddy," she said.

"That sounds like a good idea, pipsqueak," I murmured, then moved my lips an inch lower and repeated the action until she had a little constellation of purple marks on her thigh, which I mirrored on the other side.

By the time I was done, her pussy was *wet*. Wet enough that her lips were slick and if we'd been fucking, I could've just glided into her effortlessly. My cock twitched at the thought, but I ignored it as I used my tongue to connect the dots I'd left on her thighs while making my way back to her core.

"Jesus, Benny," Denise said as I dragged my tongue along her lips. "You're driving me crazy."

"Good," I said, then brought my hands up and spread her pussy lips wide open so I could see her dripping little hole.

One of those stupid thoughts went through my mind just then, the kind that almost made me let out an inappropriate laugh that had nothing to do with the situation at hand. Or, well, it kind of did, because the thought was about Rob saying his idea of oral was to just tongue-fuck his girlfriend. Though, I'd never actually... hmm.

I stuck out my tongue and swirled it around her entrance, tasting the familiar tang of her pussy juices. Denise inhaled sharply, then let out a soft moan as I worked the tip of my tongue inside her.

"Benny," she gasped. "What are you—*oh*."

Her pussy muscles twitched, tightening around my tongue, and I almost laughed in delight. It was a bit of a strange sensation, but I had to admit, French-kissing her pussy was... well...

Fun.

As was teasing her. Licking up her pussy juice and avoiding her clit with my tongue, but letting my breath brush against it. Sucking on her lips, mouthing them, finding all those sensitive little spots that weren't her clit. Gripping her thighs with my hands and listening to her moan and murmur above me.

And making her squirm.

Because I did. It was a distinct action, something completely different from anything she'd done before. Part needy, part involuntary, her thighs tightened and she wriggled from side to side, almost like her pussy was desperately seeking the friction I was withholding.

Just like Adrian said she would.

"Benny," Denise whimpered before I could react to the squirm. "I need more."

I grinned against her mound. "More of what, baby?"

"Your mouth. Your tongue. *Please* lick me. I need it."

I took a breath, inhaling the scent of her as I closed my eyes. Then, I opened them and looked up at my perfect wife, her breasts rising and falling as she panted for breath.

"I'm gonna do what I want," I told her, my voice low. "You're gonna stop me if you hate it. But if I lick you, it's because *I* want to lick you, not because you're telling me to. Understand?"

Her throat flexed as she swallowed, but she nodded.

"You trust me?"

She nodded again, and I smiled before sticking my tongue out and licking her pussy.

Actually licking it. From the bottom to the top, I dragged my tongue along her opening, slowly at first and then slower still as I got closer to her clit. I could feel her eyes on me, the anticipation quivering through her, and when I finally put my tongue on her clit, she cried out.

"More," she gasped. "Please, Benny."

I circled my tongue around it once, twice, then licked at it again. Another squirm, another moan, and then I told myself I had to try it.

I had to try the vortex.

And God, I hoped it didn't ruin all the work I'd just done.

I doubted she could see my lips, but her body tensed as I took her clit in my mouth. I glanced up to see her watching, her lip sandwiched between her teeth and her forehead creased with worry. With my eyes, I tried to tell her it was okay, that I just needed to *try* this, that the second she said stop, I'd stop.

Which apparently, she understood.

"Just be careful, please," she whispered. "Not hard."

And that's when I knew Adrian had been fucking right yet again. Someone had done this to her before and they'd done it wrong, so she thought she hated it.

But, as I added just the smallest bit of suction before using my tongue to massage her clit, we both discovered that she didn't hate it in the slightest.

"Oh fuck," she gasped, and her hips bucked forward enough that my nose brushed against her pubic hair. "Holy... holy *shit*, Benny."

I didn't stop.

I played with the rhythm, alternating the tongue-and-suction combo with a sort of suck-and-release pattern. Both seemed to drive Denise crazy, making her writhe beneath me and grab at my hair. Her fingers entwined with it, gripping hard as she thrust her hips up into my face, moaning and crying out and panting for breath. I kept looking up at her, entranced by the way she was sometimes watching me and sometimes had her eyes squeezed closed with her head tilted back.

And God, my cock was hard.

It was throbbing, almost painfully, in a way I'd never experienced while doing *this*. I mean, I couldn't confirm right at that moment, but I was pretty sure I was dripping pre-cum on the rug. I was almost considering reaching down and stroking myself to get a bit of relief when Denise let out a desperate cry.

"I need your fingers in me, Daddy," she gasped, and I groaned.

I was licking her pussy, not even touching myself, and I groaned.

Bringing my left hand up under my chin, I teased her hole for a moment before sliding a finger inside of her. Immediately, her pussy walls clamped down on it, urging me further in. I kept going deeper, kept pushing it in until most my finger was buried in her, then curled it forward as I searched for her G-spot.

When I found it, she screamed.

Like, not a scary scream. But she shouted, a stream of urgent words escaping her lips as I sucked on her swollen clit.

"Daddy," she wailed. "Yes, Daddy, right there, right—"

And I couldn't take it anymore.

I reached down with my right hand, gripping my cock and stroking hard. Pre-cum coated my palm almost instantly and I dragged it down my shaft, groaning against her pussy again as I jerked off. If someone had asked me how I could focus on anything I was doing just then, I couldn't have told them. My lips were doing one thing, my tongue another, each hand tasked with a different action to get both me and my wife off. I had *no* idea how I was doing it, but it didn't matter.

What mattered was that I was, and Denise was loving it, and I was loving it as much as she was.

"Don't stop," she pleaded. "Right there, keep doing that, and don't—oh, *fuck*, Daddy, I'm going to come on your *tongue*, Daddy."

Part of me wanted to stick my tongue inside her again and find out what it felt like to have her actually come *on* my tongue, but there was no way. One, I wasn't about to stop what I was doing when she was about to come. And two, I couldn't have. Not with the way Denise's legs were suddenly over my shoulders so she could tighten her thighs around my head, and not with the way she was pulling my hair and holding me in place, my nose and mouth completely engrossed with her.

I couldn't breathe. Couldn't think. Couldn't do anything but stroke my cock harder as my wife shattered, her orgasm shrieking out of her as she gushed against me. Her body tensed and twitched and she bucked her hips, riding my face as she trembled around me.

And I fucking came.

I fucking *came*. Like, just a few seconds after her orgasm started. I couldn't think of the last time I'd come that fucking fast, and I'd never come from giving *her* head. But out of nowhere, that tingling feeling was shooting up my shaft and my balls tightened and I was groaning out the precious little air I had left in my lungs as I shot my load.

Between coming and the way Denise was clamped around me, I was almost ready to pass out when she loosened her grip so I could breathe again. My first gasped breath tasted of her orgasm, something that was thick and distinct and addictive. I still had my hand on my cock, gripping it loosely as it softened, and I stayed where I was, my head resting on her thigh as I tried to recover.

"Sorry," she said as I caught my breath.

"Huh?"

"For suffocating you."

I laughed tiredly. "Like you could suffocate me, pipsqueak."

She giggled, then shifted. "Now you?"

"Now me what?"

"I want you to come."

"I mean, I can try to do it again, but usually it takes me a bit to get it back up."

"Again?" Denise propped herself up and I looked up to see her frowning. "Wait, did you...?"

"I hope you're not attached to this rug," I said. "There's a pretty good chance I ruined it."

The crease between her eyebrows deepened. "You... you came on my rug? Just from eating my pussy?"

"Well, I mean, I used my hand a little."

She pressed her lips together, studying me for another moment before she burst out laughing. I grinned, finally forcing myself to get up and join her on the bed.

"That was amazing," she said as I pulled her into my arms and up so we could lie down as we cuddled. "I don't know what brought that on, but whatever it was... wow. That thing you did with your... your lips and tongue? Like the sucking thing? Jesus, Benny."

Smiling, I kissed the top of her head.

The goddamn vortex. I owed Adrian a fucking case of beer.

CHAPTER ELEVEN

Halle

THE MUPPET CHRISTMAS CAROL was the superior holiday movie.

I'd fight anyone who said differently.

A Charlie Brown Christmas? Boring.

Die Hard? Not a Christmas movie. *Fight me.*

Rudolph the Red-Nose Reindeer? Horrible. That annoying little dental elf deserved to get kicked out of the North Pole, just as much as the gold-digger guy with the monster-fucking fetish. I mean, you can't tell me he wasn't trying to get with that... what did he call it, a bumble? The yeti thing.

But *The Muppet Christmas Carol* was perfect in every way. The movie had the perfect blend of wholesome kitsch and absurdity. Plus, Kermit the Frog could *get* it. And attitude aside, Miss Piggy could, too.

Although, given those thoughts, maybe I should've been less judgemental about the monster-fucker from the Rudolph movie.

That was what was going through my mind when Rob walked into our apartment after work.

"Hey, baby," I said as I tried to figure out if I was more jealous of Miss Piggy or Kermit or if maybe I just needed to go to church and bring Jesus into my life for having those thoughts in the first place. Shifting on the couch, I tugged the throw blanket tighter around me as I waited for Rob to appear in the entrance to the living room.

"Hi, Hal," he replied in a low, gravelly voice that made my stomach flutter. Moments later, he appeared, work boots off but still clad in his coveralls, the sleeves rolled up to reveal the tattoos scrawled along his hands and forearms.

There was no one in the world I'd ever been attracted to the way I was attracted to Rob. Even in his dirty old coveralls and with his cheeks red from the cold outside, my body reacted to him. He was huge—six-five, I think was officially what was on his driver's license, tall enough that he instinctively ducked under doors even though there was probably a bit of clearance on most of them—and had a broad chest and shoulders. He'd been shaving his head for as long as I'd known him, and I was one of the few people he'd told it was because he'd started balding early. Not that it mattered, because he was *damn* sexy bald.

Plus, he had the whole goatee thing going on. And the aforementioned tattoos. God, I loved his tattoos. When we'd first met, he didn't have the one on his throat; that had been a year or two after we started dating, and I absolutely *loved* driving him wild by tracing patterns along it with my tongue. And the ones on his hands, which I'd been a bit uncertain of until we were in bed a few nights after he got them and the swelling had gone down.

"See, baby girl?" he'd growled in my ear, then his hand snaked up to my throat and squeezed. "I needed to get these tattooed so you can have the pretty necklace you deserve."

I know, right? I'd almost shattered in his hands just then, before he'd even started touching the rest of me.

Rob was a collection of contradictions. Intimidatingly huge and the world's biggest softie. Gruff and grungy to the point he looked borderline dangerous, but almost stereotypically kind and sweet and genuine, the way that people both expect and don't expect guys who looked like him to be.

Until you got him in the bedroom.

That was where the hard, rough badass people thought he might be came out. That was where I got the confident, domineering side of him. Where his filthy mouth and even dirtier mind took over, and I loved every bit of it.

He was never rougher than I could handle. He wasn't the kind of person to get off on hurting someone or using someone for his own pleasure. So there were no whips or floggers or paddles in our bedroom. If I was getting spanked, it was while he was inside me, and it was only ever with his hand so he could feel my skin warm beneath his palm. There were... well, not chains, but restraints, a comfy leather set of cuffs permanently attached to our bed that I tried to remember to tuck under the mattress when we had company.

God, he was so fucking hot. Way hotter than Kermit the Frog.

"You look cozy," Rob said as he leaned against the wall of the living room. "Got your napping blanket out here and everything."

I wiggled beneath the thick sherpa blanket I'd stolen off our bed and shrouded myself with. "Well, I needed it. For my nap."

He smiled, though something seemed slightly off about it. "What'd you need a nap for? Thought you were just at Candice's place."

"Exactly." I tightened the blanket around me. "Do you know how bad of an influence your boss's wife is?"

"I have some idea."

"So then you know she made me eat way too many cookies," I said. "And drink way too many mimosas. And then I walked home with Laura, so that counts as like... exercise or something."

One of Rob's eyebrows flicked up. "Are you still feeling drunk?"

It was an odd question, but I didn't clock it.

"No," I said. "That's why I had the nap. It's the number one cure for too many cookies and mimosas."

"Good," he said. "That's good."

I frowned. "I mean, yeah, but... why?"

Rob licked his lips, then curled the lower one between his teeth in a way that made heat rush down my body and straight to my core.

"Just don't want you feeling sick or anything, baby girl," he said. "Did you eat dinner yet?"

"Does a bowl of popcorn count?"

"Was it a big bowl?"

"Huge. With lots of butter."

He half-shrugged. "I think that counts as a vegetarian meal."

I laughed. "Did you?"

"Did I what?"

"Eat dinner while you were out with the guys?"

"Sort of. It was only me and Adrian and Benny so we just split some nachos. I might make something later, but I'm not hungry right now."

"There's eight dozen cookies in the freezer you could have."

He chuckled. "Yeah, that's true. How was the cookie exchange, anyway?"

"Good," I said. "My Oreo meltaways were a hit."

"They always are," he said. "Did you talk about anything fun?"

Of course. He'd been asked Candice's little question. I bit back a laugh.

"Oh, nothing really," I said. "Just the typical stuff. Baking techniques and where to buy the best shoes and if guys like eating pussy and Mrs. Wilson's awful new haircut."

A hint of a smirk crossed his face. "Definitely interesting what you all come up with when you get together."

"Are you going to tell me who the two outliers on the survey were?" I asked.

He flicked his eyebrow up. "Why? Worried I was one of them?"

I gave him an unimpressed look. "I *know* you weren't one of them."

"Yeah, 'cause I'm always the one asking for it. Right, baby girl?"

I opened my mouth, but nothing came out. Rob's tone was casual. His face was relaxed. His arms were crossed nonchalantly across his chest. The corners of his lips were flicked up, slightly amused, but his eyes were...

Not cold. Not angry. Just... sharp.

Sharp and dark.

"I'm gonna take a shower," he said before I could say anything, then stopped leaning on the wall and crossed the short distance to the couch. He slipped two fingers under my chin and tilted my head up, pressing a chaste little kiss to my lips before straightening up. "I'll be quick. Wouldn't want to miss the end of the movie."

Then he was gone, the sound of the bathroom door closing with a conclusive bang as I stared at the Muppets on the TV.

Someone must have told him what I said.

My mouth was dry, but I couldn't make myself swallow past the lump in my throat that I thought could very well be my heart.

I felt awful about it. Candice's question had caught me off guard and the whole "he tries" thing had just... it had just slipped out. I hadn't *meant* to make it sound like Rob was bad in bed. Especially because he absolutely wasn't. Candice just had a way of pressing for information and I'd had a couple of mimosas and...

That's not to say that what I said wasn't true, because... well, it was. I hated to admit it, but he just... he wasn't good at oral.

And that was fine. It was completely fine. I'd tried to make that clear to the girls and I'd asked them not to say anything, but someone must have said something and now Rob was upset and he didn't even let me explain and...

Fuck.

Fuck.

I licked my lips, clutching the blanket around me before I took a deep breath and told myself to calm down. He was going to get out of the shower, all nice and clean and relaxed after his day at work, and I was going to explain what I'd said and what I meant and that whoever told him had obviously made a bigger deal about it than it was. And then I was going to very calmly ask him who told him that I'd said anything because I'd *specifically* asked the women in that room not to say anything, and then I was going to track whoever it was down and—

Another deep breath. Another internal reminder to calm down.

There were only two people it could have been, I reasoned. Rob had been at work all day. And after work, he'd texted me to say he was going out for a drink with the guys *from* work.

And of the women who had been at the cookie exchange, there were only two people who had partners who worked with Rob.

Candice would have never said anything to Jay. She just wouldn't have. She could be loud and bold and squeeze secrets out of people like water from a sponge, but those secrets stayed locked behind her lips. We'd been friends for long enough that I knew she wouldn't share something like that, especially because she also knew Rob and I had a great sex life. We were close enough that we'd had those conversations before.

So that left Laura.

From a logical perspective, it made sense that it would be her. We'd only just met, so I didn't know her well. Seth was the newest guy on the crew. They were both young. I mean, not like *young*-young, but firmly in their mid-twenties when I was already past the big three-zero.

But there were a few problems with that as well.

For one, I walked home with Laura. She lived in a basement suite two streets away from my and Rob's apartment building, so it made sense for us to go together. But that also meant I knew what time she'd gotten home. And I also knew she didn't live with Seth. *And* that Seth had been working.

For two, Rob had said Seth wasn't at the bar with him.

So unless Laura had randomly texted Seth out of nowhere to tell him what I said, and then Seth immediately turned to Rob and asked about it, it seemed unlikely that was how Rob found out.

Not only that, but Laura wasn't the type to do it, either. I may not have known her well, but I knew enough. She was a sweet girl who taught science at the local high school and could pound back the mimosas as fast as I could. And that meant I obviously had a huge deal of respect for her.

And because she'd pulled Seth, who was a little hottie. Rob might have been my one-and-only and Seth may have been a little on the young side for me, but I could appreciate that he was gorgeous. And Laura seemed to have gotten the kid to grow up a bit in the few months they'd been together. Which, again. Mad respect.

And after she'd admitted Seth didn't like to go down on her, I'd felt a sort of kinship with the girl. We were the two people in the room who seemed to have issues with our partners performing a successful yodel in the valley.

"Does it bother you?" I asked after we left Candice's and were walking through the thin brushing of snow on the sidewalk.

"That Seth doesn't do it?" Laura said. "No. It's his choice. It's totally fine. Like, it's not even a big deal. I don't know why everyone was saying it was a big deal."

I tried not to laugh. "I meant what we were talking about."

Laura's cheeks turned pink. "Oh. Um. No."

"You sure?" I asked, looking at her from the corner of my eye.

"I am," she said. "I was... surprised, I suppose. I didn't think I knew any of you that well yet. But it was okay. It was a lot of fun, actually."

"Except the part where you had to admit your boyfriend doesn't go down on you."

"I just said—"

"Girl. I admitted to a room full of people that Rob isn't... you know. *Great* at it." I hitched the bag holding my cookies up so it would stop sliding down the sleeve of my puffy winter jacket. "You can be honest with me."

She opened her mouth, then closed it. For a moment, she was silent, her mouth twisted to the side.

"I kind of wish he would," she finally said, her voice soft. "Go down on me, I mean."

"Have you told him that?" I asked.

She shook her head. "We talked about it once. He said he didn't like it. I didn't bring it up again. So it's not really his fault."

"Why don't you tell him?"

She turned her head to look at me. "Why don't you tell Rob he's not good at it?"

I laughed and nodded. "Touché."

"No, really," Laura pressed. "Why don't you?"

"Probably the same as you," I said. "It's not a big enough deal to bring up and potentially cause issues. I don't want to make him feel bad. And honestly? I've never come from oral anyway, so it's not like I'd gain anything, you know?" I sighed, then shrugged. "Everything else about our sex life is amazing. Like, *so* amazing."

"Mine too," she said. "So it's not a big deal, right?"

"Right. Of course."

And I think we both thought it was the truth.

We talked about other unimportant things for the rest of our walk. Once we reached her apartment, she promised to text me to let me know what Seth thought of my Oreo meltaway cookies—which I knew would be that he loved them, because everyone loved them, but I pretended I was truly curious so we had a reason to keep in touch—and gave me a hug goodbye.

Then I'd gone home, taken a shower, changed into a clean pair of panties and a t-shirt, and curled up on the couch with my napping blanket and bowl of popcorn and Christmas movies until Rob texted me to say he was going out for a drink.

Nothing about any of my time with Laura made me think she would have gone out of her way to gossip like that.

But if it couldn't have been Candice or Laura, then who?

CHAPTER TWELVE

Halle

I STARED AT THE TV as the Muppet Ghost of Christmas Present laughed heartily on the screen. The shower was still running in the background.

Maybe no one had told Rob.

Maybe I was just feeling guilty and reading way too much into what he'd said. All he'd actually said was that he was always the one asking for it. And Rob always told me I was a chronic overthinker, which was very true. So maybe...

Maybe I should just talk to him about it when he got out of the shower and we were both relaxing on the couch. He would be out before the movie was over and I could turn to him and say, "Hey, you know what the Ghost of Christmas Yet To Come and I have in common?"

Brilliant. Absolutely fucking brilliant. Just what everyone wants to do the week before Christmas: insult the love of their life's pussy-eating skills with hilarious and topical yet incredibly hurtful Christmas puns.

Before I could come up with an actual plan to bring it up with Rob, he came back into the living room and startled me.

I hadn't heard the shower turn off, but he'd obviously just gotten out. He hadn't bothered with a shirt, just a pair of grey sweatpants slung low enough that the tattoos on his hips peeked out over the waistband. Beneath the tattoos on his chest and stomach, his muscles were firm and strong—not so defined as to be intimidating, but enough that it was obvious he worked a physical job and went to the gym a couple of days a week.

It was completely unfair. Those sweatpants were the equivalent of me wearing the skimpiest lingerie I could find and putting myself in the restraints on our bed; that is, fucking *irresistible*.

And he knew it.

"What'd I miss?" he asked in a low grumble as he walked over and settled on the couch next to me.

"N-Nothing," I said. "You've seen this before."

He smirked and tugged on the blanket. "C'mon. You gonna let me get cold, baby girl?"

My breath hitched and I unwrapped the blanket from around my shoulders so I could put it over both of us. As I did, Rob's eyes flicked down, taking in the sight of me with no bottoms on.

"Maybe if you were wearing something over your panties, you wouldn't be so cold," he murmured.

"I could say the same about your shirt," I said.

He adjusted the blanket over us, then put his left arm around my shoulder as he moved in close enough that the sides of our bodies were pressed together. "I'm not cold."

I bit my lip nervously. For a few moments, we both stared forward, watching... I couldn't have even said what part of the movie it was. I was too busy trying to figure out what to say, how to tell him, if it was even *worth* saying something or if it was one of those things that I would just take to my grave because if I told him, he would—

"So that question Candice had," Rob said conversationally. "How'd that come up?"

"Um... because of my cookies," I answered.

A startled laugh jostled me. "Your meltaways? How?"

"Someone made a joke that... it was Phoebe, I think actually... Phoebe said they were the kind of cookies a guy would go down on you for."

"She thought you needed to make cookies for that to happen?"

"Well, it's not like she knows you." I swallowed hard. "But, um, since we're talking about that, I—"

"It's just the craziest thing," Rob interrupted. "How that one little question got the crew talking today. And all the different opinions and ways the guys go about it. Seth almost walked off the site when he said he wasn't into it because the rest of us are *all* about it, you know? And we couldn't believe that Laura puts up with a guy who won't go down on her."

I frowned. "I thought there were two outliers."

"Benny said he wasn't super into it, but that he very enthusiastically does it when Denise asks for it. And that's kind of funny, you know?"

"That... that he does it anyway and Seth won't?"

His arm suddenly felt very heavy around my shoulder.

"Nah," he said. "That she *asks* for it."

That word again. *Ask.*

"How is that funny?" I said.

"Well, it just got me thinking," he said, his voice still casual. "All the guys talking about how their women beg to get their pussies eaten and all that. How their partners react when the guys are down there. Making them writhe and squirm and pull their hair... when they have hair, I guess."

He chuckled dryly and I joined in, though mine was a lot weaker. The hand that was over my shoulder began to move, his fingertips walking along my bare arm below the sleeve of my t-shirt.

"And I thought, you know, imagine you were the kind of guy who just—" He tapped lightly on my bicep. "—fucking—" Another tap, a little harder that time. "—*loved*—" A third tap, the hardest of all, as he spoke that word. "—eating pussy, and you were sitting there thinking you knew how to properly *spoil* your woman with your tongue, only to realize that she never quite reacts like that."

"Rob—" I breathed.

"Imagine that," he continued. "Realizing in front of all your coworkers that she doesn't ask for it. She doesn't *beg* for it the way the others do. That after all those times you've eaten her pussy, it sounds like she might not be enjoying it anywhere near as much as she could. Wouldn't that be *such* an embarrassing way to find out you sucked at eating pussy?"

No one told him.

No one had told him what I'd said, but he'd figured it out all the same. I swallowed back my nerves, hoping he couldn't feel me tremble. "I-It would be."

"It would, wouldn't it?" he murmured. "And I thought, damn, if I was that guy, I'd be so mad. I'd think to myself, 'Why wouldn't my woman tell me that?' You know? 'Why wouldn't my woman tell me I wasn't pleasing her when she knows that's always my main goal with her?' Wouldn't you be so *mad* if it was you, baby girl?"

I opened my mouth to respond, but before anything could come out, Rob twisted, pulling the blanket away and bringing his right hand up to my throat so quickly that I almost flinched. Then his face was in front of mine, his dark blue eyes glimmering with something needy and deep and...

And *exciting*.

"It's a good thing that's not us, isn't it?" he said. "Because I'm sure my woman would tell me if I wasn't eating her pussy right."

"I t-tried to—" I gasped, but suddenly he was kissing me and his mouth absorbed what I was trying to say.

"What do you say if you want me to stop?" he whispered against my lips, his voice serious but kind.

And I knew.

We were okay.

I was okay, and I was safe with him like I always was, and the fear I'd had that he was *actually* upset about this faded from my stomach, replaced by something eager and fervent and *excited*.

"Muppet," I answered promptly, my voice squeaking out our safeword in a breathless tone.

"Good girl." His hand tightened around my throat, and then the sweetness of his voice was gone. "Now see, there was another big problem with Candice asking that damn question. Do you know what it was, baby girl?"

I shook my head. And by that, I meant that I shifted my neck in a way that Rob could feel so he knew I was saying no, since he was holding my throat tight enough that I couldn't actually move my neck. Not quite tight enough to choke me—he wasn't adding pressure yet, wasn't giving me the thrill of losing control of my breath—but tight enough that I was completely at his mercy, pinned back against the couch and in his arms.

"It was that all damn day now, I've been thinking about coming home, pinning you down, and getting my mouth on your sweet little pussy."

"Oh," I breathed.

"But you're going to ask me for it," he said. "And Halle?"

I stared into his eyes, mine wide and curious and focused entirely on him.

"You're not leaving this couch until you come on my face." He began to squeeze, began taking my breath into his hand as my heart began to race. "And I'll know if you're faking it. And if you try to, there *will* be hell to pay."

Oh God.

Oh, *God*.

Chapter Thirteen

Halle

WE WERE GOING TO be there forever.

I'd never come from oral before. It was just one of those things that hadn't worked for me. It wasn't Rob specifically—I'd never had anyone make me come like that. I liked how it felt and I would get close, but something would stop me from going over the edge each time. Between that and Rob's... um, *technique*, I guess it could be called...

I was worried.

Just a little worried.

But before I could overthink about it, Rob's lips were on mine again, stealing my ability to take in those shallow breaths of air as he slipped his tongue in my mouth. His beard was rough against my skin as he indulged me with kisses and I kissed him back eagerly until I had no choice but to struggle to gasp for breath. Just when I started to see spots in my eyes, he pulled back and let go of my throat all at once.

I gulped in a huge breath of air, gasping as I looked up at him. There was a lopsided smirk on his face as he let me breathe.

"You good?" he asked.

"Uh-huh," I replied, then remembered what he'd said about asking him. "Will you eat my pussy please, baby?"

He laughed.

He actually laughed.

"Oh no, baby girl," he said. "When I said you were going to ask for it, I meant you were going to *beg* for it. And we're not there yet."

Then he kissed me again, though he didn't bring his hand back to my throat. Instead, it moved to my thigh, cupping the side of it before dragging his palm up to my hip. There, he toyed with the band of my panties—just a simple pair of pink bikini-cut cotton ones—before trailing his fingers up my side and making me shiver.

I wasn't wearing a bra because why the fuck would I? I was at home. I wore a bra as little as possible, partly because they were uncomfortable and mainly because two years earlier, Rob had taken me to get my nipples pierced for our anniversary.

At my request, of course.

It was a long, long, *long* few months of healing time where he couldn't play with them, but it was worth it. Now, one of Rob's favourite things in the entire world was when I wore thin t-shirts with no bra so he could see the little barbells poking through the fabric.

So no bras at home had become my default.

That meant when he reached my breasts, there was nothing there to stop him from immediately cupping one of them in his large hand. I moaned as he squeezed, shifting on the couch as he flicked his thumb across my nipple, then again when he pinched it between his fingers and twisted it ever so slightly.

"God, you're so responsive," he growled against my lips. "Do you know how much I love that about you, Halle? Listening to you moan whenever you like something? It's so fucking good. So fucking hot."

"Yes," I breathed. "I know. You've told me."

He chuckled. "Good. Do it more."

I let my lips curl up into a mischievous smile. "Yes, sir."

Instantly, his hand left my breast and clamped around my throat, shoving my head back against the couch.

"What did I tell you about calling me 'sir'?" he asked coldly.

I swallowed, knowing he felt my throat flex under his palm. "Not to."

"What did I say to call me instead?"

"Rob. Or baby. But not 'sir.'"

"And what did you just do?"

I licked my lips, trying not to smirk at him. "I'm sorry, sir."

His hand tightened. "You know you can just ask me to choke you harder, right?"

"Ungh," I said, because it was the only noise I could make.

He kissed me again, then bit down on my lower lip, which made me make a strange squeaking noise. A moment later, he released my throat, replacing his hand with his mouth and kissing the tender skin along my neck.

I sighed as he did, eyes fluttering closed as he kissed his way down to my collarbone and the V-neck of my t-shirt. I shifted on the couch, moving forward in anticipation for him to tug my shirt up like he always did so he could kiss and lick and suck my breasts, but he brought his hand to my shoulder and pushed me down. Frowning, I looked down, watching as instead of stripping me, he moved his lips over the thin fabric.

His hand moved from my shoulder to my breast, squeezing it gently as he found my nipple through the fabric. Enthralled, I watched as he nuzzled the hard little nub, then nearly jumped out of his arms and off the couch as he sank his teeth into my nipple.

Not hard. Just enough that I felt it, and through the fabric, it didn't actually hurt at all. But my nipples were sensitive and the action shocked me enough that Rob glanced up with raised eyebrows, a question in his eyes as he held my nipple between his teeth.

"Again," I whispered, and I cried out when he listened.

He did it a few more times before switching to my other breast, still keeping his mouth over my t-shirt. It was surprisingly erotic, surprisingly enticing, especially when he started pinching and flicking my nipple, adding a contradictory roughness from the soft fabric.

"You have the best tits, baby girl," he mumbled as he buried his face against my cleavage. "I could do this forever."

"I thought you were going to eat my pussy," I replied.

"I said I *could* do it forever, not that I *will* do it forever," he said, then bit the side of my breast, making me squeal before I laughed.

He kept exploring me, kept teasing me, kept tracing the curves of my body and using my t-shirt as a barrier. By the time he reached my hips again, I was almost surprised at how wet I was, given that he wasn't even touching me under my clothes. But I was, and I could feel it, and as his hand slipped between my legs, I knew he felt it too.

"Look at you," he murmured. "So needy."

"I need you to eat my pussy," I said, almost hopefully, but he laughed and shook his head.

"Not until you beg, baby girl."

He traced his thick fingers along my slit, letting the cotton absorb the wetness leaking from my entrance and molding the fabric to my pussy. Then he drew in a breath, kissed me again, and moved away.

There was a slight pause where he used his foot to nudge the coffee table out of the way before he shifted off the couch, falling to his knees on the carpet in front of me. He grabbed my hips, yanked me forward so my ass was on the edge of the cushion, then placed a hand on each of my knees. I watched as he guided my legs apart, baring my still-covered pussy to him.

"You will tell me if you don't like something I do," he said.

It was an order. Not a question. But I nodded all the same. He nodded in return, then leaned forward and...

And kissed my stomach.

I wasn't quite sure why. That was not where my pussy was. But I watched as he nuzzled against it, pressing a kiss around the area of my belly button before moving his head lower, then lower again. Carefully, he moved the hem of my t-shirt up so there was a strip of skin showing just above my panties.

He kissed that strip of skin, then kept up his trail of kisses, pressing them to my pussy overtop of the fabric. I frowned as I watched, unsure of what he was doing; he'd said he wasn't going to eat my pussy until I begged for it, yet there he was, with his head and his mouth between my legs like he was about to... eat my pussy.

A few moments later, I understood.

He nuzzled against my mound, his nose close to bumping my clit, but not quite there. Then his tongue snaked out, a little harder than it usually would as he used it to mimic the way he'd traced my lips with his finger.

Then he... sort of bit me.

In a sexy way.

But not in a biting way.

I had no idea how to explain it. He used his lips to tease mine, sort of pressing down on one side and then the other in a way that was oddly thrilling considering he was... not *biting*, but... lip-squeezing? I drew in a breath and he looked up, our eyes meeting.

There was a strange look in them, at least for him: uncertainty. Something not quite confident. Not quite sure of what he was doing. Something that was at odds with the man who had just told me I was going to beg for him to eat my pussy. Something that said he'd...

Oh my God.

He'd gone out for drinks with the guys to *learn*.

CHAPTER FOURTEEN

Halle

IT ALL MADE SENSE now.

Rob had figured out that I wasn't as into it as he was. So he'd spent the night going out of his way to find out how to fix it. And now he was trying the things they'd told him to do.

Because he would do anything to make me happy. Anything to make me feel good. Because the fact that he enjoyed eating my pussy more than I enjoyed it wasn't good enough for him; knowing it didn't bring me the same amount of pleasure meant he *couldn't* enjoy it.

God, I fucking loved him.

"Do it again," I breathed.

The corner of Rob's eyes crinkled and he repeated the strange not-quite-biting action, then buried his face against my panties. I felt something press against my clit—his tongue, I was fairly sure, though with my panties in the way it wasn't quite enough to feel overwhelmingly good—and then his lips were moving again.

He kissed down my slit, then turned his head and peppered kisses along my groin and thigh. As he sucked on the tender skin there, he glanced up every so often to see how I was reacting.

And it was good. I just needed...

"Harder," I whispered.

He raised his eyebrows.

"You can do it a little harder," I repeated. "Just like—*oh*!"

The gasp came out high pitched as I felt his teeth rake against my skin. There was no way that wasn't going to leave a mark, but that didn't matter. What mattered was that electricity surged over my body from that spot, settling somewhere deep in the pit of my stomach in that place where arousal pooled and begged to be filled. Involuntarily, I shifted my hips, craving the friction between my legs that Rob was very careful not to give me.

He pressed a kiss to the spot he'd just ravished, then moved his head to my other thigh... and did it again.

And again.

"God, that feels good," I whispered, and I swear to God, he *groaned* against my leg. His hands moved up to my knees and slid along the smooth skin of my thighs, caressing them and massaging them, savouring me as he used his tongue to map little trails from each spot he sucked on.

After a while, he focused his attention back on my pussy, though his mouth was still over my panties. His left hand moved from my thigh to my hip, then slipped further up and beneath my shirt so he could grip my breast. I moaned softly as he teased my slit with his tongue, tasting my juices as they seeped through the cotton, giving me not quite enough friction to relieve the ache that was starting in my core.

"Rob," I finally said.

He glanced up.

"Please."

He raised his eyebrows.

"Please what?" he asked, and I felt the words as he spoke them against my mound.

I bit my lip. "Please eat my pussy."

"Hmm," he said, and I whimpered as the sound vibrated against me. "That still didn't sound like begging, baby girl."

"I can beg harder."

His eyes darkened. "Do you remember what I said about faking it?"

"That was about orgasms."

He glared at me. "It counts here, too."

I licked my lips, then bit the bottom one again. "Well... then... will you at least take my panties off?"

For some reason, that seemed to surprise him. Then, he smirked again. "Are you trying to trick me into eating your pussy, baby girl?"

I shook my head. "It just... I want to feel you on my skin. Please? I'll take my shirt off too. I know you want me to."

He studied me for a moment, then pressed a quick kiss to the top of my mound before nodding once.

"Improvise and adapt," he muttered to himself.

"Huh?"

"Nothing." He pulled back, peppering kisses along my thigh all the way down to my knee. "Take your shirt off, baby girl. Let me see your tits."

I lifted it obediently, wasting no time as I pulled it over my head and let it fall to the floor beside him. Rob looked up, his eyes hooded as he drank in my body, and that look alone was enough to make my pussy ache all over again. I mean, I couldn't imagine anyone *not* feeling like an absolute goddess when someone like him was looking at them like that.

I let him look for a few long moments before squirming in place on the couch.

"Baby?" I asked. "Please, will you take my panties off?"

"Mmm," he said, a low grunt that seemed to mean yes, since he brought his hands to my hips and began to peel my cotton panties down my legs.

"God *damn*, Halle," he said once he'd removed them completely and tossed them to the side. "Every moment you're not naked is a fucking tragedy."

A flattered warmth ran through me, but it didn't last long. That was only because it was replaced with the warmth of arousal he leaned forward, burying his head between my legs again, and licked a path from the bottom of my pussy all the way up to *just* before my clit... and stopped.

"No," I whined.

He put both hands on my thighs and squeezed hard. "You said you weren't trying to trick me into eating your pussy."

"I'm not," I said, but I couldn't help pushing my hips forward. "But that doesn't mean I wanted you to stop."

He glanced up at me, amusement on his face.

"So you like it, baby girl?" he asked. "You like it when I do this?"

And he repeated the same action, dragging his tongue along my slit—not between it, just overtop of it—and getting just close enough to my clit that I tensed, then whimpered as he took his tongue away again.

"I asked you if you liked it," he said.

"Yes," I said quickly. "Yes, I like it."

"Do you like this?" he asked, his voice husky as he lowered his mouth again, then repeated the not-biting action on one of my lips.

And I did. I liked it.

I nodded and he repeated the action, then moved to the other side and did it there. After that, he repeated the not-quite-between-my-folds tongue lick.

Only this time, he licked my clit.

My hips jerked forward, but his mouth was gone before it touched him.

"No," I gasped. "Rob, please."

He held my gaze as he brought his mouth back to my pussy, sticking his tongue and slowly—*horribly* slowly, *painfully* slowly—dragged it along my slit, closer and closer to my clit, until—

"No!" I cried as he avoided my clit again. I tried to push my hips forward, but he put a large hand on each one and held me down easily.

Without a word, he started the path again and I held in a breath, pleading with my eyes as he licked again, and got closer, and—

Nothing.

Again he did it, and again, and again, until I finally couldn't take it anymore.

"Fuck!" I wailed as he avoided my clit again, tilting my head back and slamming my eyes shut. "Rob, *please*!"

"Please what?" he asked.

I almost sobbed. "Please just eat my pussy!"

CHAPTER FIFTEEN

Halle

I EXPECTED THE SLOW torture again. Part of me just assumed Rob wouldn't believe I was really begging, that after all of this, he would think I was just saying it. But something in my voice must have convinced him because before I'd even taken my next breath, my clit into his mouth and he'd started sucking.

It almost knocked me off the couch.

I let out a sound that was part moan and part shriek as relief shot through me. Not full relief, of course, but that momentary alleviation that immediately demanded more, and more, and *more*. It wasn't until strong fingers wrapped around each of my wrists that I even realized I'd grabbed at Rob's head, clutching it to me until he pried my arms away so he could focus on what he was doing.

And what he was doing... Jesus fuck.

Rob's technique before had involved sticking his tongue in my vagina alternated with the occasional odd fumbling of his tongue around my clit. Not quite *on* my clit. It was like he knew where it was but had no idea what to do with it. Which was weird, because in every other situation, he knew exactly what to do with it, but for some reason, his tongue hadn't received the memo.

Now, though...

It was insane.

It was like he was a different person. My legs ended up hooked over his shoulders, my feet finding purchase against his back so I could push myself forward against his face as much as possible. He sucked on my clit, his tongue flicking against it, targeting the exact right spot to make me shiver and tremble and pant beneath him. Then he stopped, looking up at me as he released my clit before licking all the way from the bottom of my pussy like he had before, only now, his tongue was between my folds and dragged along my clit each and every time.

And *fuck*.

It was... it was fucking good.

So fucking good.

But it wasn't enough.

It felt like forever that I was in that place just before the edge, a sort of pre-orgasmic purgatory with a wall I simply couldn't pass, as much as I was desperate to. What he was doing felt amazing and part of me was straining, trying to break down that wall, wanting to scream and pound against it until I broke through and did exactly as he'd told me I would.

But I couldn't.

"Rob," I finally whimpered. "I can't..."

He flicked his tongue against my clit. "You will."

"I *can't*," I said. "It's... it's so fucking good and I want to so bad but it's... my stupid fucking body won't let me."

That was, apparently, both the worst and best thing I could have said.

Rob paused, glaring up at me with his mouth still pressed to my pussy. "Excuse me?"

"Wha—"

He let go of my wrists, which he'd been holding the entire time, and suddenly one of his hands was on my throat. He was so much bigger than me that he barely had to move, just reached up and easily clasped me by the neck.

93

"Do not *ever* call this body 'stupid' again," he growled. "This is *mine*. And it's fucking perfect." His hand tightened. "Understand?"

"Yes," I said. "I understand."

His hand tightened again and I moaned. Or, well, I tried to moan. It came out soft and strangled and urgent, but Rob must have felt it against his palm, because he groaned.

"Again," he demanded, and I made another noise that made him moan into my pussy.

Then his mouth was back on my clit, doing the sucking-and-tongue-flicking thing again, and I was lost. All I could feel was his hand on my throat and his mouth working my clit and air trapped in my lungs. I writhed beneath him, squirming, trying to get more when there wasn't even more to *get*.

Until he stuck a finger in my pussy.

He loosened his hand on my throat when he did because I gasped so hard I choked, but before he could stop what he was doing, I clenched my thighs around his head to hold him in place. I felt him react to that, though what kind of reaction was beyond me; it might have been a laugh or a moan or even a word, but I didn't care.

I didn't fucking care.

Because I was close. I'd gotten past that wall and I could see the edge now, that peak where there was nothing but bliss and pleasure and everything *good*...

But I couldn't reach it.

"Rob," I sobbed, though I didn't know if he could even hear me given how quiet my voice was and how tight my legs were around his head. "I *can't—*"

He mumbled something against my pussy, then he took his finger out of my pussy and stuck it in my ass.

I mean, he did it nicely. Carefully. He used my juices to work the tip of it in, stretching the tight ring of muscle with his thick fingertip all politely so it didn't hurt me.

At least, I think he did.

I wouldn't know. Because apparently, after years of not being able to, all it took was a hand around my throat and a finger in my ass before I was coming against someone's face. Shattering. *Falling*. It was like something had pushed me, like the Ghost of Christmas About To Come shoved me to the precipice and watched me trip over my fucking shoelaces to plunge over the edge.

And I was screaming. I think. I was making a noise, and Rob could probably feel it with his hand, but with my lack of breath and the absolute ecstasy rushing through me, I couldn't have said what that noise was. My vision was black, then white, then black again as I jerked beneath him, everything around me made of pure energy and pure bliss.

It felt like it stretched on forever. Like that moment was infinite, never-ending, like I was going to be stuck in that torturous place of overwhelming pleasure. But eventually, it faded, and I could breathe again and Rob was looking up at me. I must have let my legs relax enough that he could escape their grip or something. I wouldn't know. I was leaning heavily against the couch and I also might have been crying? My eyes were wet and I couldn't figure out why, but it didn't matter.

"Baby girl?" Rob was saying, his voice full of concern. "Halle? Are you okay?"

"Fuck me," I gasped.

"What?" he asked.

"Fuck me." I tried to sit up, but my limbs felt like the bones had all disintegrated into dust. "I need to make you come."

"Halle—"

"*Use* me, Rob," I demanded. "Please."

"Baby girl—"

"*Please*, sir," I said, and the sudden frustration with me using that word seemed to dissolve away any worries he had about me.

Which was good, because even from the pathetic angle I'd managed to pull myself into, I could see his hard cock bulging out of his sweats and an actual spot that was wet with pre-cum. He lifted himself off his knees just enough to pull his sweats down, then pulled me off the couch and into his lap. I steadied myself on his shoulders, clinging to him as he guided his cock inside me. Both of us sighed as he entered me, my pussy so wet that he was buried completely in a single thrust.

I tried to roll my hips, to ride his cock and spoil him the way he'd just spoiled me, but I was beyond that.

"Hold still," Rob growled. "Let me use you, baby girl."

I moaned and he buried his head against my neck. Strong hands gripped my hips, lifting me up and down on his cock as he chased his own release.

"You feel so good," I whispered in his ear once I'd recovered enough to think again. "Everything about you. Your cock. Your mouth... Jesus, Rob. I can't get enough of you. I want you forever, just like this."

"Fuck, baby girl," he groaned. "I want you forever, too."

"Fuck me harder," I murmured. "Fuck me and come inside me and make my little pussy all yours. Because it is, it's *yours*, baby. However you want it, for always."

"All mine," he grunted. "Fuck, Hal. I'm—*ugh*."

And then he shuddered, wrapping his arms around my waist and holding me still as he came, his cock twitching as he spilled his release inside me. I kissed his neck, his cheek, his shoulder as he did, feeling his breath warm against my skin as he held me.

"I'm sorry," he finally said, his voice soft and tired.

I frowned. "For what?"

"Not making you come again so—"

I couldn't help it. I laughed, shaking my head. "Coming like that again right away might have killed me."

He twisted his head, kissing my neck. "And for not eating your pussy right for so long."

I sighed. "Baby, it wasn't—"

"Don't. You said you tried to tell me. I didn't hear it. And I spent all this time not getting to feel *that*." He groaned, carefully lifting me off his cock so we could get back onto the couch. "There isn't anything else that you feel that way about, right?"

"Nothing at all," I promised as I curled up in his arms, then pressed my lips together. "Although I also, um, need to say I'm sorry."

"Baby girl, I just said I wasn't the one listening."

I winced. "Not that."

"Oh?"

"I... said something. At the cookie exchange."

"About me sucking at eating pussy?"

"I didn't say it like that. Not even close to that. But I don't want you to hear from someone that I did and think—"

He cut me off with a soft chuckle. "It's okay, baby. I outed myself as sucking at it in front of the entire crew today."

"I still feel bad."

"Tell you what. Make it up to me by not being mad if I tell the guys I fucking rocked this tonight."

"Done. And don't be mad if I brag to the girls that you fucking rocked it tonight."

He laughed tiredly and pressed a kiss to the top of my head. "Done."

Chapter Sixteen

Adrian

THERE WERE PROS AND cons to being the token single guy in his late twenties.

Pro: I was single.

Pro: I could do whatever I wanted.

Pro: I could do *who*ever I wanted. With consent, of course.

Pro: It wasn't a problem to stay out after work to have a couple of drinks with the guys, since I didn't have to worry about keeping someone waiting back at home.

Pro: Being single apparently gave me an edge for knowing how to please women, since I had to prove my worth to anyone I wanted to sleep with every time I wanted to fuck.

Con: My bleeding heart apparently thought that made it my responsibility to help these poor fuckers who *weren't* doing what it took to keep their partners happy, so I was stuck doling out advice and comfort like some kind of pussy-eating spirit guide.

They were lucky I was so goddamn generous.

"Well, Rob, my man?" I asked as I set my pint glass back down after Benny bowed out to go test my patent-pending and perfectly proven pussy-eating technique on his pregnant wife that he totally thought no one knew was pregnant. "Any more questions for the cunnilingus savant?"

He gave me an unimpressed look, which I took to mean he thought my comment was the epitome of hilarity.

"If not, I'm gonna head out and get ready for my date," I continued.

"You got a date tonight?" Rob asked, not even bothering to hide his surprise.

"Yeah. There are a few hot singles in my area who want to send me nude photos right now, no credit card required." I lifted a hand to catch the server's attention, mouthing the word 'Bill?' at her. She nodded and turned to the computer, and I turned back to Rob. "Now. What's still bringing you down, my dude?"

He hesitated, then shook his head. "I'm kinda pissed at her."

"Who? Halle?" He nodded and I stared at him, bewildered. "Why?"

"Because she didn't tell me."

"... that you weren't doing it right?"

"I mean, yeah." He fidgeted with his pint glass. "If I sucked so badly at it, why the hell didn't she say anything?"

"Are you sure she didn't try?"

"You saying I don't listen to my woman?"

I shrugged. "Pobody's nerfect."

"The eighties called. They want their catchphrases back."

I smirked. "The nineties called. They want that lame-ass joke back."

He laughed, which I figured was a good sign that he wasn't going to kill me for insinuating he wasn't nerfect. The server picked that moment to show up with the bill and I grabbed it, shaking my head as Rob dug in his pocket for his wallet. I paid, left a decent tip on account of the fact that I was fairly sure we'd scarred her with our conversation, then waited until she walked away before I put my elbows on the table and leaned forward.

"Look, Rob. Maybe Halle tried to tell you and maybe she didn't. If she did try, cut yourself some slack. You're doing what you can now to correct it. It's not like you're, you know... Seth or something, refusing to even try. And if she didn't try to tell you, cut her some slack."

His jaw twitched. "I just don't get why she wouldn't talk to me. Like, fuck. How goddamn embarrassing to find out five years into our relationship, in front of all the guys at work, that she doesn't like what I'm doing?"

I tilted my head thoughtfully, the corners of my lips pointing down. "I mean, yeah. It was embarrassing. But hilarious. I'm not planning on ever letting the day you blurted out 'I think I suck at eating pussy' in front of the entire crew fade from my memory."

"Thanks," he said dryly.

"You're welcome. But seriously, dude." I gave him a meaningful look. "Don't be pissed with her."

"It's not like I'm going to fight with her or something. It's just—"

"It's just nothing. Look, if you take *anything* away from our talk tonight, make it that eating pussy is complicated." I clasped my hands together as I leaned on the table. "Some women don't like it. Some love it. Some want it just as foreplay. Some want to come. Every woman is a little different. And the same techniques and shit won't work for every woman. I mean, hell." I shook my head, laughing softly. "The same techniques might not work for the *same* woman every time. What Halle likes one day might be totally different the next time. That's not her fault. That's just fucking biology or something, man."

"Yeah, but—"

"But nothing." I tapped my fingers on the table. "Even *trying* to communicate what she wants or doesn't want or what's working or what's not working is hard. Maybe if you were with someone else, but I've met Halle. I don't think her not telling you is about *you*, you know? Your sex life is good otherwise?"

He nodded.

"Then good." I sat up straight and flipped my palms up casually. "Don't be pissed at her because this one thing isn't working out right now. You know there's a problem. Now it's up to you to solve it."

"And how am I supposed to do that?"

I rolled my eyes and stood up, grabbing my winter coat and shrugging it on. "Seriously, dude?"

He looked up at me blankly. "What?"

I sighed. "Rob. Robbie. Robert Robinson Robsley the Third. Did you listen to a *single* fucking word I said tonight?"

"Yeah, but—"

"Then take my fucking advice, go home, and eat her goddamn pussy until you figure out what *she* likes!" I stood up and clapped Rob on the shoulder. "Thank me later. You can pay me back with a nice bottle of bourbon."

And with that, I left the bar, intent on finding me some totally-not-a-bot babes to chat with for a while.

But as I got back to my place that night, one of the major cons of being single made itself known. Mainly, that I'd spent the whole fucking day talking and thinking about eating pussy, and there were absolutely no hot singles in my area trying to send me no-credit-card-required nudes.

Not that the nudes would have helped.

No, I was in one of those agitatedly horny moods when I got home. You know the type. It was the kind of mood where even after I got home, got into the shower, and shot a load out before even washing my hair, I didn't feel... you know.

Satisfied.

It wasn't even that I'd wanted to bust in someone's mouth or pussy or even for it to be someone else's hand. What I wanted was to get *my* mouth on a pussy and just fucking...

Just fucking indulge. Just lick and suck and play with a swollen little clit, feel someone gush against my face, feel her grab my hair and grind against my tongue. I wanted the warmth and wetness and salty-sweet scent and tangy taste.

And all I had was my own fucking hand.

Still, I tried to trick myself into thinking it was enough. After I soaped up and rinsed off, I got out of the shower and put on a pair of sweats and a t-shirt, then went over to my bed and grabbed my laptop. For a while, I tried to find something to watch: a movie or a new episode of the sci-fi drama I'd gotten into or even, God forbid, a stand-up comedy special.

But what I was looking for wasn't on any streaming service or TV channel. What I wanted to watch was a woman as I made her come with my tongue.

Con of being a single guy in his late twenties: trying to find someone to let me do that.

Because as much as I might be a master of eating pussy and an all-around great catch for any woman wanting a night of feeling like an absolute goddess, picking women up in a small town like Southbush wasn't the easiest feat. There was really just Whiskey Sours as far as nightlife went, and that made it a lot harder to find someone to hook up with.

Not impossible.

But nowhere near as likely.

Especially, I told myself, being right before Christmas. People were already off of work for the holidays, heading out to their family events or to last-minute Christmas parties. Even my parents had plans that night; Dad might've been Hindu, but he got as much into the Christmas spirit as my raised-Catholic-but-hadn't-been-to-church-for-years mother did. Nadia had told me they were going into Calgary for the weekend to see the Christmas lights and go to some event with a bunch of other retirees like them.

But, I mused as I scrolled through pages of movie suggestions simply to give my hand something to do that wasn't sticking it down my pants, maybe I would get lucky. I mean, I couldn't be the only single person left in Southbush a few days before Christmas.

Before I could overthink it, I got out of bed and changed into jeans and a long-sleeved Henley shirt. Then I scrubbed my face with the stupidly overpriced face wash I would never admit to using because toxic masculinity prevented me from admitting that my *sick* skin care routine is what gave my skin its soft and healthy glow, applied more overpriced creams and oils and cologne, and half an hour later, I was walking back into Whiskey Sours.

CHAPTER SEVENTEEN
Adrian

To no one's surprise, the bar was not busy. I surveyed the other patrons and flagged exactly one potential person who may be interested in having her pussy tongue-bathed until she couldn't remember her own name: a tall, slim woman sitting at the bar, her long, dark hair cascading down her back and nearly blending in with the all-black ensemble she had on. She was facing away from me, of course, so I couldn't tell what the front of her looked like, but the back was perfectly enticing on its own.

The bar stools on either side of her were empty. As were the ones beside those, which was even better. But before I could start towards one of the empty stools, my eyes fell on a familiar face sitting by himself.

I almost walked past him.

Because frankly, I'd been generous today already. I'd shared my patent-pending techniques with both Rob and Benny, bolstered Rob's confidence, and honestly? I was going to claim responsibility by association for the earth-shattering orgasms both Halle and Denise were probably having right at that very moment.

I'd been more than generous and it was time for me to spoil myself a little.

I started towards the bar, but before I got even three steps closer, some unknown force made my feet turn towards the table. Probably some fucking Christmas ghost that was trying to earn its wings by making me teach other men how to ring their woman's bell.

It could've been that I was feeling kind of guilty for inappropriately insinuating I'd eat out his girlfriend if he didn't have the balls to do it when he was clearly upset about us calling him out for not having the balls to do it.

But it was probably the goddamn piece-of-shit ghosts.

Resigned to my fate to be the Jacob Marley to the poor little Scrooge McFucker sitting at that table, his face solemn and lost as he stared into his pint glass, I sighed and pulled out the chair across from him. It was only as I sat down that he finally looked up and noticed me.

And he groaned.

"Seriously? What are you doing here?" Seth asked.

"Good to see you, too, dude," I said, shrugging my wool peacoat off. "And what do you mean, what am I doing here? You knew I was going to be here. I invited you for a drink with me and Benny and Rob after work."

"That was hours ago," he said, his voice flat. "I would've thought you'd already left."

"Well, I came back."

He made an unimpressed noise. "Look, no offense, but you're the last fucking person I want to see right now. Can you just pretend you didn't notice me and just go do whatever drew you back to this shithole?"

"Seth, baby, if I could, I would," I said. "But something tells me the Ghost of Not Being Able To Make Your Girlfriend Come has drawn me here to provide you aid this very eve."

"Fuck you," he said.

"Flattered," I said. "Especially coming from a verifiably handsome dude like yourself. Alas, I'm not into people currently invested in long-term relationships, so no, but thank you."

"No, I meant—" He sighed and rolled his eyes. "I can make my girlfriend come just fine, thank you."

"Not with your mouth."

"I am so sick of this goddamn conversation," he muttered.

"As am I, especially since I'd like to take care of my own needs tonight at some point," I said. "So let's get to the bottom of this quickly."

"Bottom of what?" he replied. "No one asked you to help me get to the bottom of anything."

"Well, someone has to," I said. "You're sitting in a bar by yourself on a Saturday when you have a perfectly good woman at home to enjoy the company of."

"We don't live together."

"Semantics, Sethly Setherson. You know what I mean."

He tilted his head back, closing his eyes briefly in an attempt to quash what I assumed was annoyance for me. But after looking back at me and opening his mouth, nothing came. Instead, he hesitated, then took a deep breath and let it out.

"Laura and I kinda had a fight," he said.

"Because you don't eat pussy?"

"Will you drop the pussy-eating thing?" he asked, a little louder than was strictly necessary. "That's... I mean, yes, that's part of it, but it's not... the whole thing."

"But it's why you're upset."

"It... maybe." He sighed. "I wasn't going to say shit about it but I couldn't fucking stop thinking about that goddamn question after I got home. So after I showered and ate dinner, I texted Laura."

I winced. "Ooh. Text fights. Never a good strategy."

He looked at me, unimpressed. "I just asked her how the cookie exchange was at first. If she had fun and how the cookies were and to save some for me, you know? And it was fine. Then I asked her about the question. Just a general, you know, 'what brought that on' sort of thing."

"Alright," I said, nodding supportively. "Alright, alright, alright. No screwups yet."

He glared at me. "So she tells me, and we're kind of texting back and forth about how crazy it was to talk about that with a bunch of women she barely knew, and then I... I asked her."

"Asked her what?"

"If it bothered her that I don't go down on her." He twisted his pint glass in his hand. "It took her a while to text back. Like, normally Laura responds right away. And I could see that she'd read the message. Finally she texts back and she's like, 'I don't want you to feel like you have to do things you don't like just for my pleasure.'"

I let out a low whistle. "Oh, boy. She was trying real hard not to hurt your wee little feelings. So she does want you to go down on her."

"She said she's into it but that she respects that I'm not." He stared at his beer, then took a sip. "And yeah, it upset me that she didn't... I mean, I thought it wasn't a big deal and now I'm finding out it is. Like, I'm sitting there wondering if she thinks I'm selfish because—" He stopped and sighed again, the sound agitated. "I don't ask her to go down on me. She does and obviously I like it, but it's not like I'm *asking* 'cause I know that's not fair. She said she does it because she likes doing it. But what if she thinks I think eating pussy isn't 'manly' or whatever? Which I don't... or, well... Like, it has nothing to do with manliness or anything, but knowing she might think of me like that is..."

"I mean, I get it, but that's a little, uh..." I twisted my wrist in the air as I tried to think of a nice way to put it, then failed. "... oversensitive-egotistical-crybaby of you."

He opened his mouth, disagreement written across his face, then just sighed and shook his head. "You don't need to point out that I'm a fucking moron. I texted her back and she didn't reply right away, and when she did, it was in her teacher voice."

"I thought you were texting."

"Well, yeah, but you can tell," he said as if it was the most obvious thing in the world. "She gets all diplomatic and proper. Like—" His voice went high and bitter as he mocked Laura's voice. "'I can see we're both reacting strongly to this situation right now and we each have feelings that are very valid, Seth. Perhaps this isn't a conversation that's best suited for text messages.' So I said fine, I'd talk to her some other time, and then I decided I needed a beer and came here."

"You know she's right."

"Of course I know she's right!" The anger in his voice didn't match the look on his face, which was something almost remorseful. "I'm just... I got defensive. Because I thought she'd be mad. But Laura's not like that. She's sweet and understanding about shit like this."

"So why don't you just have an actual conversation with her about why you don't want to do that for her?"

"Because she... she wouldn't actually understand."

His voice was serious enough that I didn't make fun of him. His words came out in that sad, dejected sort of tone that wasn't just mopey or dramatic, but legitimately unhappy in a hopeless sort of way.

"Look, buddy," I said. "This fight isn't going to end your relationship. What you need to do is finish that beer, then sit down and have a good, long think about why you can't tell your very smart, very sweet, very mature and understanding girlfriend about whatever is causing this aversion to pleasuring her with your mouth. Then, once you've gathered those thoughts up, you know what you do?"

"What?" he asked.

"Really, Seth baby?" I asked.

"Let me guess," he said. "I should just be a man, suck it up, and go down on her?"

I pinched the bridge of my nose. "God, why is everyone so stupid?" Straightening up, I leaned forward. "Seth. You go *talk* to her. And don't forget to apologize."

"Oh," he said. "I mean, yeah. I know."

I sipped my water, then set the glass down on the table firmly. "Bud, I'm not gonna pretend I understand why you won't do it for her. You're talking to the wrong person for that part of it because frankly, I came back here for the *sole* purpose of trying to find someone I can practice my tongue twisters on. Personally, I think it's an experience every guy should indulge in. But if you can't see that you're missing out on—"

"You all seem so fucking sure that it's because I don't *want* to," Seth interrupted.

I stopped, mouth still half-open.

The man had a point. I had very much assumed that it was because he didn't want to. Mostly because I couldn't think of a reason that he wouldn't do it otherwise.

But I could be wrong. That was an unlikely, but not impossible, option. And if I *was* wrong, that made me even more of a dickhead for what I'd said earlier. No wonder he hadn't wanted to see me.

"Alright, that's fair," I said. "So I don't know if it's a confidence thing or a physical thing or what, but regardless, Laura's opinion is the only one that matters."

He sighed, then lifted the pint glass to his mouth and drank the last of it before setting it down. "You're right."

"Oh, God," I fake-moaned. "Say that again. It really does it for me."

"Fuck you, Adrian," he muttered, twisting in his chair to flag down the server.

"Normally I'd let you buy me a drink first," I said as I stood. "But this time it's on me."

"Huh?"

"I'll get your tab. *Mea culpa* for earlier today. Go home and call your girl."

"Oh. Uh... thanks. That's nice of you."

"Yeah, I know. Don't tell anyone about it or they'll think I'm getting soft." I clapped a hand on his shoulder. "Good luck and see ya tomorrow, man."

There. I'd done my good deeds for the day. Hopefully, karma would notice and swing things in my favour when it came to the hot-from-the-back woman who was still sitting at the bar with two empty bar stools on either side of her.

CHAPTER EIGHTEEN
Adrian

As SETH HEADED OUT, I went up to the bar. The bartender was the same as the guy who had been there earlier: a tall, Latino guy with short hair and thick eyebrows that were currently furrowed as he noticed Seth leaving.

"He's not drink-and-dashing," I said as the bartender put down the glass he'd been wiping and started towards the exit.

"'Scuse me?" the bartender said.

I slid onto one of the bar stools, leaving an empty one between me and the woman in black, not looking at her. "He's a buddy of mine. Had a rough day, you know? A fight with the old lady. I was just reminding him how good he has it and how that amazing woman deserves the best of the best. He wanted to make it up to her as quick as possible, so I said I'd cover him this time."

The bartender glanced at the door, then at me and shrugged. "If you say so, man. I'll add you to the same tab."

"You're a gem, my friend." I leaned on the bar, then turned my head casually towards the woman I'd been eyeing. "What are you drinking?"

She looked at me, raising her eyebrows as I took in my first look at her from the front.

The good news was she was even *hotter* from that angle. I didn't recognize her from anywhere, which wasn't unusual; Southbush might be a small town, but it wasn't like everyone knew *everyone*. A green bejewelled clip swept the aforementioned long, black hair off her pale pinkish-white face and she had large, round, hazel eyes. She wore red lipstick and the black outfit that had looked so elegant from the back was even better from the front: a black blazer overtop of some kind of lacy black top tucked into fitted dress pants.

"Me?" she asked.

"Uh-huh." I tilted my chin towards the rocks glass in her hand. "What's that?"

"I don't need another one," she said.

I shot her a smile and shook my head. "I mean, I'd be happy to get you one, but I meant for me."

That seemed to catch her off guard. "What?"

I shrugged. "I don't know what I'm in the mood for. So what're you drinking?"

"Oh," she said, glancing down at her glass. "It's, um, an old fashioned."

"Oooh." I didn't even need to fake the low, soft groan of appreciation that came out of my mouth. "Yeah, that's one-hundred percent what I'm in the mood for." I glanced at the bartender, who had a cautious look on his face. "One of those, please."

"You got it, man," the bartender said.

As he turned to grab a glass, I smiled at the woman. "Great suggestion. Thank you."

"No problem," she replied.

And then I ignored her.

It wasn't like it was some kind of game. Not really. Like, I guess one could argue that it *could* be a bit of a game, but that was only if I was doing it for nefarious reasons, which I wasn't. So it wasn't until the bartender set my drink in front of me and walked away to take an order from someone sitting at the other end of the bar that we spoke again.

"Does this usually work for you?" she asked.

I took a sip of the drink and savoured the smooth burn of the bourbon before looking at her. "Does what usually work?"

"The 'I'm a nice guy who's just innocently asking you for a drink recommendation and am totally not hitting on you' schtick."

I laughed and shrugged. "I mean, I guess, if by 'schtick' you mean I was legitimately asking you for a drink recommendation."

"Right. So you weren't hitting on me?"

"Not that you're not completely worthy of hitting on, but no, I wasn't."

Her lips parted, then she glanced down. "Oh."

I glanced at the bartender, who was still busy at the other end of the bar, then leaned towards the woman, though the empty stool between us kept a respectable gap.

"I was gauging if you were interested in chatting with some random stranger," I said, lowering my voice a bit. "Which could have very, very easily turned into me hitting on you. When you said you didn't need another drink, I assumed you weren't into it, and I didn't want to ruin your night by not taking the hint. But I am *more* than happy to be told I'm wrong."

She held my gaze for a moment, silently assessing me. Then, she pressed her lips together and twisted on the stool so she could hold out her right hand to me.

"I'm Olivia," she said.

I put my glass down and shook her hand. "Adrian. At the risk of sounding like I learned how to talk to women from a 1960s magazine that I definitely only read for the articles, what's a gal like you doing in a place like this all by yourself?"

Her red-painted lips twisted, trying to hold in a smile. "A 'gal like me'? What's that supposed to mean?"

I picked up my drink, leaning on the bar as I took a sip. "Well, it's a Saturday night just before Christmas. You're all dressed up, but here on your own. Could be that you're here for a mundane reason, like being stood up by some asshole who doesn't know what's good for him. Or..." I trailed off, then shrugged. "Something far less traumatic than that."

She laughed. "Well, I don't know about *less* traumatic, but I didn't get stood up. I thought I'd stop by for a drink on my way home from work."

"Rough day?"

"I work at the mall."

"That explains the trauma."

She shrugged. "It could be worse. I work at Lacy Pleasures."

I had no idea what that was, but nodded like I did, which didn't fool her.

"The lingerie store," she said.

"Oh," I replied. "Yeah, I can see that being a little stressful the week before Christmas."

She nodded. "Not as bad as some places, but we get our share. Most our gift-seekers at this time of year are panicked husbands who don't know what size their wife actually is, but assume we can figure it out by them gesturing with their hands as they try to describe what it feels like."

"Yikes. You sure you don't want that second drink? Maybe a third?"

She laughed and shook her head. "I just need the one to decompress. After my sister stopped by and—" She cut herself off, her cheeks turning a delightful shade of pink as she glanced around quickly, then leaned closer towards me. "She bought herself her very first set of lingerie."

"That's..." I started, then shook my head. "I have no idea how to respond to that."

"What's your instinct?" she asked.

I shrugged helplessly. "Nice of you to help her, maybe? Either that or weird, I guess, that she bought her first set of lingerie from her sister. But also, I'm not sure if I'm supposed to be picturing your sister in lingerie."

"How would you... You don't even know my sister."

"In my imagination, you're twins."

Olivia's laugh was loud enough that the bartender glanced over. "Think you're pretty good, do you?"

"I think I'm very good," I said. "But when I'm bad, I'm better."

"You're really into the whole vintage pop culture, aren't you?"

"Mae West always has been and always will be an absolute goddess."

She rolled her eyes, but that smile didn't leave her lips. "Well, it was a bit weird, but not *that* weird. Just odd to feel like my little sister is growing up."

"How old is she?"

"Twenty-seven."

I burst out laughing. "I mean... yeah. I'd say she's grown up."

"Yeah, but if she's grown up and I'm her older sister, that means *I'm* grown up," Olivia said, then took a dramatic sip of her drink. "And I can't possibly be a grown up. I'm too young."

"You're what, twenty-two?" I asked.

"Flattery gets you nowhere," she replied. "I just said I was older than she was."

I held my hand up in surrender. "Fine, fine. I aimed a bit under. You're clearly twenty-two and a half. But you don't look a day over twenty-five."

Flattery did appear to get me somewhere when she laughed again.

"Anyway, it was great to see Phoebe with her friends and all, but spending all that time off the floor put me behind and apparently, every granny in Southbush wanted to come in today for her BBB."

"BBB?"

"Basic Beige Bra." Olivia sighed and sipped her drink. "You'd be surprised how picky they get about something that is literally basic and beige. And then this woman tried on a lingerie set from one of our new designers and it was just *horribly* constructed. I felt so bad. We try to only bring in designers who have inclusive sizes but this was just—" She stopped and shook her head. "She was so nice about it, but agh. I felt terrible. Between that and the guy who yelled at me for telling him there was no way his wife was a 36C if most of her t-shirts were an extra-small, then the lineup of people who didn't seem to understand that 'closing time' does not mean 'grab yet another bra to bring into the fitting room time,' I figured I deserve a drink. And since my roommate isn't home, I decided to do it here so I didn't feel like I was drinking by myself. Plus—" She sipped her drink again. "—Miguel makes a far better old fashioned than I do."

I mirrored her action, swirling the bourbon in my mouth. "That he does. This is great."

"The secret ingredient is maple syrup." She tilted her glass towards me. "Instead of simple syrup. Don't tell him I told you."

I mimed zipping my lips shut.

"So what about you?" she asked.

"What about me?" I replied.

"What's a guy like you doing in a nice place like this?"

I chuckled. "Just stopped in for a drink."

"Really?"

"Of course."

She shook her head. "Liar."

I tried to look affronted, but I was laughing too hard. "Why would you say I'm a liar?"

She pursed her lips, her eyes sparkling as she crossed one leg over the other. "Come on. Give me some credit here."

I glanced at the bartender, then looked back at her.

"You really want to know?" I asked, my voice barely above a whisper. "'Cause this is either gonna get me slapped or it's totally going to work."

"Now I'm even more intrigued."

I took another sip of my drink, then set it down on the bar.

"Okay," I said, still looking down at my drink. "Here's the thing." I looked up at Olivia, catching her eye. "You ever have a major craving that you just can't get past? One of those things that you're thinking about *all* day and no matter what you do, you can't stop thinking about it? And you know the only thing that'll make that craving go away is getting that specific thing?"

"I suppose," she said suspiciously, keeping her voice as quiet as mine. "What is it you're craving so specifically?"

Raking my teeth over my bottom lip, I glanced down at her mouth, then back up at her eyes. "I've been dying to eat pussy all fucking day."

I think Olivia thought she knew what I was going to say; that is, a lot of fancy words to tell her I was horny and wanted to get laid. But she didn't seem to expect that response. Her eyes widened and she blinked, her lips parting in surprise.

"Have you?" she asked.

I nodded. "It's all I've wanted for hours. All I can think about is how much I want to bury my face in someone's pussy and just go to town."

"Oh," she said.

"So," I said. "Think you can help me out with that craving?"

A hint of sass crossed her face. "What makes you think I want to sleep with you?"

"As much as I'd fucking love that, I'm not asking you to." I lifted my glass, but didn't take a sip of it. "I want to go down on you. You wouldn't have to reciprocate or get me off in any way if you didn't want to. I just want to make you come on my face and then if you want me to fuck off, I'll fuck off." I tilted my glass towards her. "The caveat being that I will absolutely jack off to the memory of it when I get home."

She stared at me, her lips still parted as I finally took a sip of my drink. The tension between the two of us was thick, but I was happy to let it hang there for a moment as she processed what I'd said.

Apparently, however, the tension was noticeable.

"Everything okay over here?"

I looked up as the bartender approached, his eyes hard and his voice a low rumble as he looked from Olivia to me.

"Wonderful," I said. "This is an excellent old fashioned, man. You make a hell of a good drink."

He nodded at me in a way that made it very clear he was not actually asking *me*. "And you, Olivia? Everything alright?"

"Everything's great," she said, her voice quiet but genuine. "Thank you for checking. I think we're both fine, though."

His nod to her was a lot friendlier, somehow. "Let me know if you need anything."

"So, let me get this straight," Olivia said as the bartender walked away. "You just... want to go down on me."

"Yep."

"No strings attached."

"None at all."

She pursed her lips. "So if I send you away when I finish, you'll go home and masturbate to the memory of it, but you're completely fine with that being the only thing you get out of this encounter?"

"Correct."

"And what makes you think I'm just going to let some strange man come back to my place to go down on me? What do I get out of this?"

"Off, obviously," I said.

"Huh?"

"You get off." I grinned at her. "I mean, you had a rough day at work, right? What better way to relax at the end of it than let someone else take care of you and make you feel good?"

"And that's *really* all you want?"

"I promise," I said. "I'll give you my phone number, my address, my full name, whatever info you want to show you I'm not just some creep. But I swear, all I want is to eat your pussy. I just..." I shook my head, closing my eyes briefly. "You have no idea how much I fucking love it."

Olivia was quiet for a moment. Then, she tapped her fingers against the bar.

"See him? The bartender?" she asked, tilting her head towards him.

"I do," I said. "He's a big dude and I'm just a little guy. He could totally kick my ass."

"That's Miguel. He's pretty much my brother-in-law. He'll know I'm leaving with you. So if you try anything, he'll hunt you down."

"I would expect nothing less," I said.

"And I have a roommate. Who will be home at an undisclosed time."

"I completely understand if they burst in to check on you," I said. "Since I'm fully planning on making you scream my name. It's Adrian, as a reminder."

She picked up her glass and downed the rest of her old fashioned. "Let's go, then."

CHAPTER NINETEEN

Adrian

AFTER I PAID THE bill, Olivia drove us to her apartment. It wasn't that far from Whiskey Sours, which was good, since if I was super fucking lucky and she let me stay the night, I'd be able to walk back in the morning to pick up my car before work. Not that it ended up mattering; as soon as we pulled into the parking lot, I spotted Rob's truck parked in one of the stalls near the entrance and could've probably just bummed a ride from him.

Small towns, man.

The apartment Olivia led me to was on the fourth floor and faced away from the parking lot. She unlocked the door and flicked the light on, illuminating a decent-sized two-bedroom that looked like something off a design blog. Muted grey fabric covered the furniture and a mix of textured throw pillows were arranged on the couch. In one corner of the living room, a decorated Christmas tree was twinkling merrily, and in the other, a tall bookshelf showcased carefully curated knick-knacks and potted plants.

"Nice place," I said as I took off my jacket.

"Thanks," she replied, motioning to the hook on the wall for me to hang my coat. "It's my roommate's doing. She wants to be an interior designer."

Then, that moment of awkwardness, made even more awkward because I'd told her it didn't have to be a typical hookup and that meant we probably weren't starting off the way most hookups did.

Namely, by making out.

"Can I get you a drink or something?" she asked.

"Nah," I said. "You can show me to your bedroom, then tell me if there's anything off-limits before I start licking your pussy."

She giggled nervously. "What do you mean, off-limits? I thought you just wanted to eat me out."

I smiled, leaning against the wall in the front entryway as I folded my arms. "Well, yeah. But there are still... you know. *Levels* of that. Like, can I get you fully naked or do you want to limit it? Do you just want me to focus on your pussy or can I touch other parts of you? Is there anything you really, really hate and don't want me to do?"

"I... I don't know," she said. "I've never had a hookup like this before."

"That's okay," I said reassuringly. "There's no rush. And also no pressure to continue if you don't want to. You're in charge here, Olivia."

She nodded, still looking uncertain, then took a deep breath and squared her shoulders.

"My room is the second door on the left," she said, motioning to the hallway. "Go wait for me there. I'm going to freshen up in the bathroom and then I'll... I'll answer your questions."

I did as she said, letting myself into her room and settling on the edge of a neatly made queen-size bed to wait for her. Her room was cozy and clean, everything tucked away in its proper place. I was idly looking at a photo on Olivia's dresser of her with a gorgeous chubby girl who looked a lot like her when she returned to the room a few minutes later.

She'd shrugged off her blazer, leaving her just in black dress pants and the lacy fitted top that was tucked into them. Her hair brushed along the pale skin of her shoulders and upper arms, a dark contrast that made every inch of her look mouth-watering.

"Wow," I said.

She smiled as she closed the bedroom door behind here.

"You can undress me," she said. "You can touch and kiss other parts of my body if you need to. Don't leave any marks or hickeys. I don't mind anal-related things, but seeing as we've just met, I don't think I want to go there tonight."

"Understood," I said.

"Don't slap me, hit me, call me names, or hold me down," she continued. "Not that you have any reason to, but I don't want you to touch my feet. And—" She cleared her throat, a blush of pink rising from her throat up to her cheekbones. "—I think it would be best if you kept your clothes on for now."

"Understandable, of course," I said.

Her face turned red. "Not that you aren't hot, but I... I think that would help me stay relaxed in this whole ridiculous situation."

I chuckled and nodded. "You got it, baby."

She wrinkled her nose. "And don't call me that."

"Yes, ma'am."

That made her giggle again and I grinned, standing up and moving off the edge of her bed.

"Anything else?" I asked.

She shook her head and I licked my lips, finally letting my eyes trail down her body and really *drink* her in.

"Why don't you take off your pants and lie down however is comfortable for you?" I said.

"Just my pants?"

"For now." I smiled at her. "I want to unwrap the rest of my gifts later."

She rolled her eyes, but unbuttoned the waistband of her pants and slid them down her hips. That was when I realized it wasn't actually a *top* that she was wearing; it was one of those bodysuits that kind of looked like a one-piece bathing suit.

My breath hitched as she stepped out of her pants, leaving her pale body clad just in black lace. I watched as she got onto her bed, flashing her ass cheeks at me as they peeked out of the thong back. My dick started to stir, a slight throb of awareness as Olivia settled on top of the covers and propped herself up on the pillows. Once she stopped moving, she looked up at me expectantly.

As confident as I was when it came to eating pussy, there was always that moment of nervous excitement before diving in. I licked my lips, indulging in the anticipation and reminding myself that I knew exactly what I was doing before moving forward to join her on the bed.

I think, even given all my assurances, Olivia was skeptical of what was about to happen. I couldn't blame her. Part of me was surprised that any of this had even worked at all. But that assumed skepticism just made me even more determined to prove to her she'd made the right choice in inviting me back to her place.

To start, I put my hands on her shins. Her legs were silky and soft and I slowly slid my palms up towards her knees. Keeping my gaze locked on hers, I slipped my hands to the inner side of her knees and slowly nudged them apart so I could take my place between them.

"You good, ma'am?" I asked.

She laughed again and nodded. I smiled and parted her legs further, only then letting my eyes trail down her body and between her legs.

I'd seen these bodysuit things in, like, porn and stuff before, but I'd never hooked up with a girl who was wearing one. I had no idea if they were all as fucking sexy as the one Olivia was wearing, but damn, was this one ever hot. The thing was lace from top to bottom, slightly sheer and showing peeks of her skin through the thinner parts of the fabric. She had a bra on, so I couldn't see her nipples, and there was a band of what was probably cotton or something on the crotch of the suit. Two tiny silver snaps winked at me from there, the only thing that was holding it all together. Like a thong, the back of it disappeared between Olivia's ass cheeks, while the front of it was already showing the folds of her pussy through the fabric.

God, I loved the shit women wore. This was one of the hottest things I'd seen in my life, and my dick throbbed its agreement.

"You're fucking sexy," I said.

"Apparently," Olivia replied. "But I didn't bring you back here just to stare at me." She looked at me pointedly, then parted her thighs even further. "*Someone* insisted he wanted to eat me out."

"*Someone* knows we always eat with our eyes first," I replied.

Before she could say anything else, I lifted her leg so I could hook it over my shoulder, turning my head and kissing the side of her calf. She made a soft noise and I continued, closing my eyes and indulging in the salt smoothness of her skin. My tongue snaked out occasionally as I kissed my way up from her calf to her knee.

Then I lowered myself, moving onto my stomach so I was positioned between her thighs in a spot where I could access every bit of her body that I needed to. Once I was, I slipped my hand beneath her other leg so I could guide it over my shoulder, then resumed my path of licks and kisses up the inside of her thigh.

Her breath quickened as I got closer to her pussy. So did mine, in fairness; by the time I was almost at her groin, I could smell her arousal through the thin fabric of her bodysuit and my dick was almost at full-mast, as eager as I was to find out what she tasted like.

But I didn't dive in right away. Of course I didn't. I mean, I'd barely started. I still had to unwrap her.

So instead, I disappointed my dick by leaning forward and pressing a kiss to her stomach through the lacy bodysuit. I spent some time peppering kisses along the spot where the waistband of her panties would be, if she were wearing any, before moving my head to her other leg and kissing down her thigh towards her knee.

"You have fantastic legs," I murmured as I lingered at a spot mid-thigh that had made her inhale sharply.

"I do a lot of walking," she replied. "Retail, you know."

"Mmm," I said, then sank my teeth into the spot I'd been kissing.

What? She'd said no marks and no hickeys. She hadn't said a fucking *word* about biting.

So I nibbled gently on her thigh, drawing a high-pitched gasp from her before releasing the spot from between my teeth and soothing it with a soft kiss.

I spent a bit more time kissing her legs and thighs before moving my head back to her core. Taking a moment to indulge myself, I pressed a gentle kiss against her fabric-covered pussy before sitting back so I could bring my hands up to the snaps on her bodysuit.

"Still okay?" I asked as my fingers brushed against her pussy.

"Still okay," she said.

"Good," I said, and then I completely fumbled those goddamn snaps as I tried to undo them.

It should have been simple. They were snaps. Not hooks. Not buttons. Not a goddamn combination lock. *Snaps*. It should have been a quick tug of the fabric and then bam. Pussy.

But instead, Olivia giggled as I tried to pry them apart.

"I thought you wanted to unwrap me," she teased.

"I do," I said, trying not to grit my teeth. "But this is like when someone ties a knot in the ribbon on a present."

She burst out laughing and began to reach down, but before she could nudge my hands out of the way, the snaps came undone with a soft click and the fabric separated.

"There," I said, resisting the urge to let out a cheer of accomplishment.

"Good work," she said.

"Thanks." I pushed the bodysuit up, distracted by the sudden revelation of her pussy. I stared for a moment, then felt a slow smile spread across my face as I glanced up at Olivia. "That'll be the only thing I fumble. I promise."

"So you're leaving the bra hooks to me, then?" she asked innocently.

I tried to glare at her, but her playful smirk just made me laugh. So instead, I peeled the bodysuit a bit higher up her stomach, then dipped back down and ran my tongue along her slit.

CHAPTER TWENTY

Adrian

OLIVIA JUMPED SLIGHTLY, GASPING in surprise as I dove into her pussy.

Which was fair. I'd told the guys earlier to start by teasing, to tongue at all the folds and tease the entrance and take their time tasting and touching and tantalizing.

But I'd also told them to improvise and adapt.

I didn't need to tease Olivia. She was already curious. Already excited. Already wondering and anticipating what was going to happen, and she had been from the moment I'd sat next to her at Whiskey Sours. And I'd told her what I wanted, that I was craving *pussy*.

Teasing her would just be tormenting myself, really. Especially after seeing her revealed to me. Like, I'd seen my fair share of pussies, but hers was just...

God, it was beautiful.

Her lips were a little puffy, but not overly so; just a perfect peach shaved bare, save for the tidy strip of hair on her mound. Though, I doubted she *shaved*; the skin there was too smooth and perfect to be just shaven. And then, poking out from between her lips, that perfect little bundle of nerves that I would be lavishing for most of the night. It was already a bit swollen, begging to be licked and sucked from its place at the top of her slit.

So instead of teasing, I dove in, making out with her pussy and coating my tongue with the wetness already leaking from her entrance. She tasted sweet and tangy and slightly soapy in a fresh sort of way that I couldn't get enough of.

Slipping my arms beneath her thighs, I reached up for her waist, gripping it and pulling her body down towards me before sinking my tongue between her folds greedily. Olivia moaned, then shifted beneath me. I glanced up to see her lifting the bodysuit over her head, leaving her in just her bra.

It was a fabulous view, of course, but it didn't last. Almost immediately, she slid her hand behind her back and unhooked it, the cups falling away from her tits, then shrugged it off and tossed it to the side.

And that view was just fucking *exquisite.*

Olivia's tits were beautiful. Like, absolutely glorious, to the point that I almost regretted not starting up there. Her nipples were tiny and pale pink, hard little nubs at the peak of breasts that were probably a perfect handful. Between that, the flavour of her sweet little pussy, and the way I was lying on the bed, when my cock twitched beneath me, I couldn't help but let out a muffled noise of pleasure.

She blushed and bit her lip, but I could see the smile beneath it as she reached down and ran her fingers through my hair.

"You really do like eating pussy, don't you?" she murmured.

I answered by taking her clit into my mouth and sucking on it, making her cry out and squirm beneath me. And, as everyone probably knew, I was a big fan of women squirming when I ate them out, so that made me groan my appreciation against her pussy.

My dick was throbbing in my pants, pressing hard against my jeans and pinned between my body and the mattress. As I moved my hands to Olivia's thighs to keep her spread wide for me, she brought her hands up to her breasts and squeezed them, enraptured as she watched me spoil her swollen clit. Almost unconsciously, I pushed my hips forward, grinding against her bed and indulging in the pressure against my cock.

I didn't know if she could tell I was almost humping her mattress, but it didn't seem to matter. Olivia's breathing was already coming faster as she played with her nipples, pinching them between her fingers while I tongued her pussy. I made another noise against her, closing my eyes and releasing her clit from my mouth so I could lap my tongue up and down her folds, rubbing her clit against it each time I reached the top of her pussy.

The first time I got there, she cried out, and when I repeated the action a few moments later, she thrust her hips up against my face. I moved my hands from her thighs to her hips, not to hold her down but to support them as she pushed up into my mouth, grinding her clit against my tongue.

"That's so good," she gasped. "Fuck, that's…"

And she trailed off into a moan as I tried not to ruin everything by letting my mouth twist up into a grin. She let go of one of her breasts and brought her hand down to my head, running her fingers through my hair again before steadying her palm on the back of my head for leverage.

We kept going like that for a while, Olivia rolling her hips and using my tongue wantonly. She had one foot pressed against my back, her head tilted against the pillows as she took her pleasure from my mouth.

And I could have left it there. I could've made her come like that. She was settled in, comfortable, the bed frame squeaking as she worked her hips against me. Her movements were enough that even I was feeling pretty good, since her bed was gently bouncing against my cock. Sure, it wasn't enough to make me come, but it felt good and she could've easily gotten off, too.

But that's not how I rolled.

I slid one of my hands back under her hips and wrapped it around her, letting my palm rest against her stomach so I could keep her leg pressed against the side of my head. Then, I brought my other hand up beneath my chin.

She whimpered as I moved my mouth away from her pussy, but I worked quickly, licking my middle finger and getting it nice and slick before twisting my wrist so I could work it into her needy hole.

"Oh, *fuck*," Olivia gasped as I penetrated her, and then she shrieked as I moved back to her clit and took it into my mouth again.

Her hips pushed up again, but this time it was just because she was arching her back as I began to finger her. I barely had to curl my finger before finding her G-spot; her slick walls were tight and hot and eagerly accepting my finger into them.

"Oh, Jesus," she moaned, which was great timing, since I needed to give my jaw a slight break. I lifted my head away from her pussy.

"It's Adrian," I reminded her. "Jesus is coming next week."

Her laughter was breathless and staggered with moans as I kept sawing my finger in and out of her.

"You... are... awful," she giggled.

I raised my eyebrows. "I mean, I can stop if you think—"

"Your humour is awful!" she blurted quickly. "Don't you dare stop and leave me on the edge like this."

I grinned, then quickly worked my jaw from side to side before lowering my lips back to her pussy.

"Yes, ma'am," I murmured, and then I started lavishing attention on her clit again.

She cried out, writhing beneath me as her back arched off the bed again, her legs trembling around me. My finger was still inside her, still pressing against her G-spot when I felt her reach down and grab not my head, but the hand I had resting on her stomach. I lifted it and she entwined her fingers in mine, gripping it tightly as she began panting harder and harder.

"Don't stop," she pleaded. "Oh, fuck, please keep doing it just like *that*, Adrian... Adrian, fuck, I—"

She cut herself off with a screech and I moaned into her pussy, my eyes squeezing shut as the sound of her calling my name seemed to shoot straight to my dick. It throbbed, but I ignored it; as much as I wanted to hump against her bed in a pathetic attempt at release, Olivia was bucking beneath me and I knew what that meant. I knew what the tightening around my finger meant, what the noises meant, what the sudden tension in her body meant.

Especially when she screamed it.

"Fuck, I'm coming," she gasped, then another loud moan. "Don't stop, I'm coming, don't stop, don't—*ahh*!"

And oh, God, was she fucking phenomenal when she came.

I mean, not to brag, but I'd made a lot of women come with my mouth.

Okay, maybe that *was* a brag.

But Olivia coming like that was easily one of the best things I'd ever seen in my life. The noises she made, the way her tits were thrust in the air, the feeling of her hand gripping mine and her pussy gripping my finger, the way her pale skin flushed red all across her chest...

Fuck.

She orgasmed in a way that made being single seem like an absolutely shit situation.

My cock was throbbing. Aching. So hard that it felt like my skin was stretched as tight as it would go. I was so fucking turned on, so goddamn horny, so desperate to put my dick in *something* that I almost couldn't think.

And yet, all I wanted was to do that to her all over again.

So I did.

I doubt she was expecting me to. I think she thought I was just lapping at her pussy because her thighs were so tight around my head, but when she tried to let her legs fall open, I moved my hands beneath them and held them in place.

"Oh my God," she whimpered, and the next noises that came out of her mouth were barely coherent.

It took a little longer to make her come that time, but that was okay. At first, she twitched beneath me, her hips jerking as I carefully teased her oversensitive clit, my tongue feathering across it lightly until she relaxed enough to stop trembling beneath me. Then I alternated between licking her pussy, sucking it, and rubbing her clit as I kissed her thighs to give my jaw a break when I needed it. She reached down, running the fingers of one hand through my hair as she kept her other fingers entwined with my one hand.

I got her to come the same way as the first time, with my finger curled against her G-spot. That orgasm seemed to hit her even harder, if the way she bucked her hips and pulled my hair was any indication.

Which I figured it was.

When she was done, she collapsed back against the bed, gasping for breath as the tension in her body released and her legs fell away from my head. This time I let them, working my fingers out of hers as her grip on my hand loosened. She let go of my hair as I pulled my finger out of her pussy. A breathlessly dejected noise left her mouth as I did, though it faded as she watched me bring my finger to my mouth and lick it clean.

"Oh my God," she murmured. "You are *really* good at that."

I tried not to look arrogant, but it was hard when I really was that good at it. "Thank you."

She laughed and closed her eyes, resting heavily against the pillows. While she caught her breath, I wiped my sopping face with the sleeve of my shirt and discreetly adjusted my dick, which was screaming painfully for attention. I glanced at Olivia, trying to gauge if she was interested in more, but her eyes were still closed, one arm resting above her head and the other across her ribs.

Which was fine. I wouldn't have said I was okay with dining and dashing if I hadn't *actually* been okay with it.

Leaning down, I pressed a chaste kiss against one smooth thigh before slipping off the bed. It wasn't until I was standing that Olivia opened her eyes, looking up at me curiously.

"What are you doing?"

"Uh... getting ready to go?" I said.

"Why?"

"I mean, I did say that you could tell me to fuck off when we were done and I'd fuck off."

"And did I tell you to fuck off?"

"Well..."

She propped herself up on her elbows, frowning at me. "You think you can make me come like—make me come like that *twice*— and just walk away?"

I tried not to laugh. "I didn't want to presume."

Rolling her eyes, she sat up and curled her legs under her. "Do you like blowjobs, Adrian?"

"Does the Pope shit in the woods?"

She frowned. "I don't know. Does he?"

I shrugged. "I have no idea. I'm not Catholic. Or the outdoorsy type."

Laughing, she shook her head, then crawled towards me. "Remember when you said I had no idea how much you love eating pussy?"

"I... may recall saying something like that."

She was at the edge of the bed now, kneeling in a way that brought her face in line with mine.

"Well," she said. "You have no idea how much I *love* sucking cock. And I'm pretty sure I can get two out of you, too."

Then she grabbed the front of my shirt and tugged me forward to kiss me.

CHAPTER TWENTY-ONE

Seth

SOMEONE WAS GONNA CALL the RCMP on me if I didn't decide what to do soon.

Not that I'd blame them. In fact, should someone look out their front window, notice some random dude had been sitting in his turned-off car on a snowy street in the dark for a while, and *didn't* think it was suspicious, I'd question their judgement. Sure, I wasn't doing anything wrong, but it wasn't like this hypothetical person would know why I was there. And then I'd have to explain to a cop why I was sitting there shivering with a sad-looking cupcake and an overpriced Elf on the Shelf replacement doll.

Which wouldn't go over well, because I was parked by my girlfriend's place and once I'd explained *that*, they'd probably think I was trying to intimidate her or something. Then they'd go talk to Laura, who would probably be in her pajamas already, and come to the door with bedhead and an adorable look of confusion on her face.

And making her get out of bed just to come to the door and talk to the cops was downright rude of me.

So, I reasoned, I should just get over it and go to her door, which had been the intent the whole time. But instead, I was frozen in the car, and not because of the cold.

Because of Adrian, that stupid, annoying little fuck.

In fairness, I liked the guy just fine most days. Most everyone on our crew got along well, which was why I was still working there. When Dave and Jay had hired me, it was just supposed to be a temporary thing during their busy season. Spring and summer, mainly, and then I'd get laid off in the fall, at which point I'd end up going back to the grocery store that always seemed to hire me when I was between better-paying jobs. But then I'd actually started working and it was like something clicked.

There was Jay, the somewhat gruff guy who was like the crew's dad. He'd taken it upon himself to teach me as much as he could, treating me like I was more than just a general labourer barely getting his feet wet in the construction industry.

Rob, who was like a cool older brother, a bad influence who had no problem showing up when he was needed, like when Laura told me some of her students were harassing her and he came with me to pick her up from school one day so those little fucks understood who they were fucking with.

Benny, a chill, easygoing guy who was like a ray of fucking sunshine in a way that was so wholesome, it was impossible to hate him.

Kendra, the sister I'd never wanted and who could be counted on to say the dirtiest things anyone could ever think of.

Adrian, the egotistical jokester who only gave you a hard time if he actually liked you, even if sometimes he took it way past the point of what was acceptable like he had that day.

And me. The new guy. The youngest one. Who had less to offer than everyone else, but tried to make up for it by working hard and being a decent person.

The work itself was okay, but what I enjoyed was the people I worked with, which was a new experience. And maybe if I hadn't met Laura, things would've gone as planned. I tended to bounce from job to job, not because I kept quitting but because I was purposely picking temporary shit. That way I could work my ass off to save up a bunch of money, then take some time off to piss that money away until I had to call the grocery store and ask Mike if I could pick up a few shifts to pay my rent so I didn't have to move back in with my parents.

But when I ran into Laura again, everything changed.

She was too good for me. I knew that. Everyone knew that. I was a mess of a person. Twenty-five with no real direction, alternating between working and partying, trying to find meaning in a life that had existed on the more chaotic side of mayhem. Suffering from growing up as the kid that could do whatever he wanted, whenever he wanted, with no consequences. The absolute last person a smart, ambitious, put-together person like Laura should involve herself with.

But she had.

Somehow, the kind of woman who would move to a small town by herself to take up a job no one else wanted—teaching science to high school kids who had been told their whole lives that there was no value in education because people who worked jobs that required math were pansies that were too good to get their hands dirty, like I had—wanted to be with me.

Somehow, a woman who knew what she wanted and how to get it decided that *I* was what she wanted.

Seeing her at the grocery store that day had felt like a sign. It was a Friday, I remember that, and I was planning on driving into Calgary that night to hit up the clubs, drop way too much money on overpriced beer, and maybe get laid. So I'd gone to the store intending to buy Gatorade and crackers for when I was inevitably hungover the next morning, and there she was, dressed in a modest navy-blue dress with her blonde hair pulled back and wire-framed glasses perched on her nose, not paying attention as she wandered down the cookie-and-cracker aisle and nearly running me down with her cart.

"Oh my God," she'd gasped, stepping around her cart with an apologetically distressed look on her face. "I'm so sorry. I was looking for the Oreos and—" She stopped and frowned. "Don't I know you?"

She did. And I knew who she was instantly. There were enough women on my body count list that I cringed when I thought of it, knowing that I could barely remember half their names and may not have ever even known some of them.

But I knew her.

I'd never forget her. Not meeting her that night at the club, or the shine of her eyes, or the way her hips had moved when she was dancing. I wouldn't forget the sounds she made when I fucked her, how I'd climbed into her bed thinking it would be a typical drunken hookup only to find myself clutching her, sighing as I took her slowly and sweetly and intensely.

And there was no way I'd forget the next morning, spooning with her, rubbing my cock against her ass until she rolled over and slung her leg over my body. The way her ass fit into my hand as we moved together in that odd position where I was half on my side and half on my back, and she wasn't quite on top of me but could roll her hips to take my cock over and over again...

She was beyond unforgettable.

I'd gotten her number and tried to keep in touch. I did. We texted for a while, but between living in different places and the fact that I was a literal mess of a person who knew she deserved better, I... well. I didn't push her away. But I didn't encourage her, as much as I couldn't get that night with her out of my head.

And there she was, standing in front of me at my local grocery store after ramming a cart into my leg.

I should've known everything had changed when I could've said something vague, like "Huh. You do look familiar…" or "I was just thinking the same thing. Did we go to high school together?" and chose not to. When, instead of trying to play it cool, I pretended the spot on my thigh that she'd rammed her cart didn't hurt at all—which was thankfully not as difficult as it would have been if she'd been about three inches to the left—and smiled.

"You're Laura," I said. "I'm Seth. We, uh… met before."

Recognition dawned on her. "Oh, yes. We… we did." Then, the recognition faded and a look of excitement took its place. "Wait, do you live here?"

"No, this is the grocery store," I said. "I live in a house."

She laughed and my entire body felt warm. "I meant in Southbush."

"Yeah," I said. "What are you doing here?"

"I live here now!" she said. "I took a teaching job at the high school a few months ago and—"

"Can I take you out to dinner?" I blurted.

She stopped talking, her lips slightly parted. "Like… on a date?"

"Yes. Unless you're, uh… seeing someone else."

"No, I'm not seeing, um, anyone." Her cheeks turned a beautiful shade of pink. "I… sure. I'd love to go out with you. When?"

I glanced at my watch. "Right now?"

"What?!"

I put the box of crackers I'd grabbed back on the shelf. "I mean, I'll help you finish your grocery shopping first if you want."

Part of me wanted to convince myself I'd done it because there was a better chance of hooking up with Laura again than picking up some random girl in Calgary. That part of me was an asshole, not to mention a fucking liar. The truth was that I took one look at her and something told me not to let her go ever again.

That she was the one.

She was worth cleaning my act up for. Worth not going to Calgary and partying all the time. Worth approaching Jay near the end of the summer and asking if he'd consider keeping me on the crew, only to feel a wave of relief as he laughed and had said he'd been planning to ask me if I'd be willing to stay on permanently.

I tried to keep that past part of my life separate from Laura. It wasn't like I lied to her about it or anything; she knew I used to be a bit of a player and that I'd been into partying and shit. I was honest about that. She deserved honesty, just like she deserved peace of mind; that second one was why I'd gone and gotten an STI test done as soon as we were exclusive. I just wanted to show her a recent one so she felt safe with me, even though we always used condoms and I knew I didn't have anything. And I'd told her about job hopping and not really knowing what I wanted to do with my life.

I wanted to prove to her I was responsible. That she wasn't making a horrible mistake by deciding to be with me.

But I didn't get into all the details with her. The whys and the excuses and the justifications. And that was why I was sitting in front of her house with that stupid fucking cupcake and creepy elf doll that had seemed like such a good idea at the time.

It had seemed so simple when Adrian told me what to do while we were at the bar. Go talk to her and don't forget to apologize. Two easy steps.

Until I got in my car and thought maybe I should bring her something. You know. Like flowers. Something to show her I really meant it and that I was thinking about her and that I felt awful for being a... what did Adrian call me? An oversensitive egotistical crybaby.

So I drove to the grocery store first, grimacing apologetically at the cashier as I walked through the door five minutes before close. I still knew some of the staff there, but she wasn't one of them, so she gave me that fake-cheerful dead-eyed smile as I rushed towards the flower section.

Where there were exactly two bouquets, both half-dead, and that looked like they wouldn't make it ten seconds in the cold winter air.

Panicked, I looked around for another solution. There were a few Christmas toys, including the Elf on a Shelf doll, so I grabbed that because... I mean, it seemed like a better option than a mini Tonka truck. And candy would have probably made more sense than a cupcake, but there was a flower decoration on it and I thought... you know. It *had* a flower, so it was like flowers, but it wasn't flowers...

God, I was fucking this up and I hadn't even started to apologize yet.

CHAPTER
TWENTY-TWO
Seth

AFTER PAYING AND PRETENDING I didn't notice the judgemental look the cashier gave me at the very odd and pathetic assortment of items I had, I jumped back in my car and drove to Laura's, my heart pounding the entire way. Once I'd parked, I took a breath, trying to figure out how to say what I needed to say. Then I'd gone to grab the cupcake and stupid elf, freezing as I looked at my sad little offering and the spiral of thoughts about how I was not at *all* good enough for Laura started all over again.

And now I'd been sitting there for a suspiciously long time.

She'd been so excited about the cookie exchange. Even though she'd lived in Southbush for a few months before we saw each other and we'd been together for about six months now, Laura hadn't made many friends. Not because she was unlikeable or something; it was just hard to make friends in a place like this as an adult, especially when the majority of people she was meeting were her students' parents and so... you know. Not people she wanted to hang out with.

So at the Christmas party, when Candice had basically taken Laura under her wing and insisted she come to the cookie exchange, she was over the moon and past all the stars.

Somehow, neither of us had known that a cookie exchange was where women drank lots of mimosas and talked about sex for hours. And for some reason, they'd talked about eating pussy and whether or not guys liked it, and that had led Candice into texting Jay and Jay asking the rest of us what we thought, and I had to sit there looking like a fucking jackass as everyone else admitted they couldn't get enough of it.

Then, instead of just letting it go, I went and made everything worse by asking Laura about it and getting mad when she was honest with me. I threw a tantrum, pouted, and now I was sitting there trying to talk myself out of apologizing because I didn't have flowers and had bought her a creepy doll.

She deserved better.

Sighing, I forced myself to pick up the cupcake and the elf. Laura deserved the best of everything. I couldn't give that to her, but at the very least, she deserved my apology for being a jackass. And maybe...

I mean, the gifts I brought were terrible, but I could always...

My stomach curled, but I tried to suppress it.

I could always go down on her, I told myself. In fact, that was what I *should* do. Because I...

I wanted to make her happy.

The more I thought about it, the more I convinced myself I could do it. I could go through with it. I had my reasons for not wanting to, but Laura was more important than those reasons.

Laura was the most important thing in my life.

"Fuck," I muttered, then took a deep breath.

I could go in there, take her to her bedroom, and lick her pussy.

I could do it.

I had to.

It still took me another minute to draw up the courage to actually open the car door, but once I did, I moved quickly. It was cold out and I hated being cold. When I was working, it didn't seem so bad because we were moving all the time and I had clothes that were graded for the weather, but I wasn't wearing my work jacket or gloves or anything that night. So I shivered and closed the car door, mashed the remote lock until my headlights flashed, and hurried down the sidewalk to Laura's place.

She lived in the basement suite of a house, but there were outdoor stairs leading to her own separate entrance. As I walked down them, I could see the golden light filtering through the frosted window in her door, so at least she was still awake. Swallowing nervously, I ran a hand through my hair, thought through what I wanted to do one last time, then adjusted how I was holding the cupcake and squared my shoulders before knocking on the door.

It took a moment before I saw movement behind the glass, which was fair. It was relatively late and I hadn't told her I was coming.

"Who's there?" she called out in her sweet, polite voice.

"Just me," I said.

She didn't answer right away and I felt my stomach knot, worried that she wouldn't answer it at all. But the outline of her body shifted through the glass and a moment later, the lock clicked and she opened the door.

The image I'd conjured up of Laura in her pajamas while talking to the imaginary cops wasn't too far from the truth. In my head, she'd been in one of those matching flannel sets, the kind that buttoned closed in the front and had a sort of lapel thing going on. And her hair had been messy, the way it was when we woke up after spending the night together.

Her hair wasn't a mess because she probably hadn't been in bed, given that the TV was on in her living room. She *was* wearing that kind of flannel pajama shirt... and that was it. It was a bit too big for her, just long enough that it covered the panties I assumed she was wearing underneath.

Every thought I'd had flew out of my head as I looked at her.

"Seth?" she asked after a moment.

"I... uh..." I said, then blinked and forced myself to look up from her legs to her face. "Sorry."

"It's okay," she said. "What are you... you know. Doing here?"

I blinked again, then shook my head. "Because I'm sorry. For being a little bitch earlier." I held out the cupcake. "I wanted to get you flowers, but they didn't have any. So I thought this, you know. Had a flower on it." I lifted the elf up and grimaced. "And then I thought, like, a teddy bear or something, but... this was all they had."

She stared at the elf doll, then pressed her lips together. Her cheek twitched the way it did when she was trying not to laugh.

"Which I'm also sorry about," I continued. "Because this thing is really fucking creepy."

She nodded as she reached up and took it from me. "It really is."

Then she glanced at me, stifling a laugh, and a wave of relief washed over me.

"The cupcake might be good though," I said.

"Thank you," she said, a giggle escaping.

I chuckled, then cleared my throat. "I really am sorry, Laura. How I acted earlier was shitty."

"It's okay," she said, reaching out to touch my arm, and even though I was wearing a thick jacket, the feel of her hand sent a warm wave of relief through me. "I accept. But, um, do you want to come in? Just, it's a little cold to stand here talking and I don't have pants on."

"I may have noticed that," I said, glancing down again.

She laughed and tugged on my sleeve. "Come in."

The door had barely swung shut when I dipped my head down and kissed her. She smiled against my mouth, reaching up to cup my cheek as she kissed me back. More importantly, she didn't pull back while I kicked my shoes off and put the cupcake down on the table by the door and tried to shrug my jacket off, instead deepening the kiss enough that I felt my cock begin to stir.

Which was good. Because if she was kissing me like that, she would probably be okay with me doing other things, and I was going to lick her pussy.

I was going to do it. As part of my apology.

And it was going to be fine.

"Have one more thing for you," I murmured against her lips, hoping my nerves didn't show.

Laura pulled back and looked up at me, her eyes wide. "You do? What is it?"

I didn't respond, just hung my jacket on one of the empty hooks by the door, then turned to Laura. Leaning in, I kissed her again and waited until she was kissing me back before moving my arms down in one smooth motion so I could pick her up.

She squealed as I did, her legs wrapping around my waist and her arms around my neck to steady herself. The squeal was followed by a thrilled giggle, one that I felt against my mouth as she grinned. I wanted to smile back, but the nerves in my chest wouldn't let me, so I just kept my lips on hers as I carefully navigated us through her basement suite to her bedroom.

Once we were there, I put her on the bed, urging her back until she had no choice but to lie down with me nestled between her legs. I kept kissing her, kept trying to hide my worries and tell myself I wasn't afraid or nervous or anything like that as I brushed her hair off her face.

I was going to do this.

Steeling my resolve, I pressed a final kiss to her lips, then moved my mouth to her neck. I nuzzled there for a moment, lifting a hand to her breast and cupping it through the flannel pajama shirt. She sighed as I did and I sucked on her neck, not hard enough to leave a mark but enough to make her shiver and shift beneath me.

Then I brought both hands to the front of her shirt and started unbuttoning it, hoping she didn't notice that my fingers were shaking as

I undid them one by one. I let my lips trail down her chest as I revealed more and more of it, kissing her collarbone and then the tops of her breasts until I'd unfastened the last button and let the shirt fall open, revealing her gorgeous body.

Laura's breasts were huge. Like, far bigger than people would expect. She dressed to minimize them, partly because she worked with teenagers and partly because she just tended towards clothes that balanced her proportions. So it was almost a surprise when she was topless and those incredible, gorgeous, firm tits were revealed.

I'd dreamed about fucking her tits multiple times. Not that I'd told her or ever asked to do it. I might one day, maybe, but it felt like one of those things that could go a few different directions when it came to her opinion of it. She might be into it or neutral about it, or she might be disgusted that I wanted to rub my cock in her cleavage and come all over her neck and chest.

Either way, it didn't matter just then. Tonight was about her. About proving myself to her. So I lavished my usual attention on her tits, burying my face against them and sucking on her nipples and tracing my tongue on the undersides of them in the way I knew would drive her crazy. As I did, I moved my hand down her body, slipping it into her panties.

She was just starting to get wet, her pussy not soaked but radiating that telltale warmth that said she was on her way there. I stroked one finger along her slit, gently exploring her folds. My thinking was that if I could get her at least partway to coming before I lowered my mouth to her pussy, it would be a lot easier.

I definitely wasn't, like, procrastinating or anything.

Once I felt her wetness coating my fingers and she began to squirm beneath me, I knew it was time. Her breasts were rising and falling as her breath started coming faster, and if I didn't do it now, chances are I never would. Taking a last indulgent moment with my face buried in her cleavage, I slipped a finger inside of her and thrust it in and out slowly, making her moan as I began to press kisses lower and lower on her torso.

I'd kissed my way to her belly button when I felt gentle fingers running through my hair.

"What are you doing?" she asked softly.

I didn't look up at her, just kissed the same spot I'd been at before. "You know what I'm doing."

"You're... going down on me?"

My stomach turned.

"Yes, baby," I said.

She was silent. I pressed another kiss to her stomach, but she didn't let go of my hair.

"Seth," she finally said. "I don't want you to."

CHAPTER
TWENTY-THREE
Seth

SHE DIDN'T... *WANT* ME to go down on her?

I looked up at Laura, stunned. "But you said... when we were texting, you said—"

"I don't want you to do something you don't want to do," she said, her eyebrows furrowed in an expression that almost looked like pain. "It's not going to make me feel good to know you're hating every second of it."

"I won't hate every second of it," I said.

"We literally argued about this earlier today."

I swallowed, trying to clear the lump of unsettled worry that had started bubbling up in my throat. "I want to be able to do this for you, baby."

"But I don't want you to do it for *me*," she said gently. "Not when I know you hate doing it."

I closed my eyes. I wasn't sure why. Maybe because that lump in my throat was still there and I felt like I was going to cry.

"Seth?" Laura said after a moment.

"I don't hate doing it," I said, keeping my voice low and controlled. "It's just..." I stopped and sighed, then looked up at her, hoping she could see me pleading. "Just let me do it for you. I want to make you happy."

She studied my face, then moved her hand to my cheek and caressed it.

"You do make me happy," she said. "And what would make me happy right now would be if you could tell me why this is something that bothers you. Then, if you still insist that you want to, we can talk about continuing."

Fuck.

I'd been hoping to avoid that.

The whole "tell me why this bothers you" thing, that is.

Because to tell her that, I was going to have to tell her everything, since that was where it stemmed from. And then she was going to wonder why I hadn't told her before. And I was going to have to explain myself, to tell her I just wanted her to see me as normal, that I hated thinking about that part of my life and hated it even more now that I had *her* and this... this relationship that meant everything to me.

But she was asking me directly. I wasn't going to lie to her or hide it from her. The only reason she didn't know was because it was one of those things that never came up. I wasn't going to volunteer the information if no one asked for it, and no one ever thought to ask about it.

And if anyone was going to be understanding, it was Laura.

Sighing, I sat back, kneeling on the bed in front of her. She adjusted, sitting up and resting against her pillows as she closed the front of her pajama top.

Great. I wasn't even going to get to look at her boobs while I did this.

"I have to tell you something before I can explain that," I said, not looking her in the eye.

The tension in the room was suddenly so thick, I almost couldn't breathe.

"Okay," she said.

"When I was a kid—" I started, then stopped to clear my throat. "I had cancer. As a kid."

The tension vanished.

"Seth," Laura breathed.

"When I was twelve," I said, still not looking at her. "I went through all the treatments and shit, got the whole Wish Mission experience. We went to Disney with my parents and got a bunch of horseback riding lessons, for some reason. And then I beat it." I laughed dryly. "Obviously, since I'm here."

She made a noise that was like a laugh. One of those sympathetic ones where neither of us found it funny, but she had to respond somehow.

"But no one ever talks about what happens after a kid beats cancer. They get spoiled. Because like, you almost died, right? So adults give you whatever you want and you turn into this total asshole because no one likes saying no to kids who had cancer." I sighed. "I know now that I was kind of a brat and I think people probably assumed I would grow out of it as I got older. Which was fair. And I probably would've, except when I was eighteen, it came back."

"Eighteen?" she repeated. "Seth, that was just a few years ago."

"Seven years," I said. "So I was back to being a cancer patient, and it fucking sucked." I shook my head. "All my friends were partying and going out and getting girlfriends and I was bald, missing my eyebrows, and puking my guts out half the time. I spent more time with my mom driving me back and forth from Calgary for appointments and shit than I did doing anything else."

"That must have been hard," she said.

"Yeah. Except somehow, I still managed to get a girlfriend." I laughed, shaking my head. "Her name was Amanda. We'd gone to high school together. She was always nice to me, but it wasn't until after I got sick again that we started spending more time together. She'd volunteer to like, bring meals over and stuff. And honestly, she made everything a lot easier to handle. She'd come to my appointments sometimes, but I'd refuse to see her for a couple of days after getting chemo because I was so sick. Other than that, it was a pretty normal relationship. We'd go to the movies or whatever. That kind of thing. But no sex."

"Oh," Laura said. "Is that normal?"

"It wasn't like, 'Oh, I have cancer, I can't have sex' or anything. More a preference thing on both our parts."

"Was she your first?" she asked.

I shook my head. "I'd hooked up with this other girl I knew before I got diagnosed. But while I was getting chemo I just felt shitty all the time, so I didn't want to. I started seeing it like this goal, almost, I guess. Like, once I beat cancer again, Amanda and I could have sex. And—" I took a deep breath. "—more specifically, I could go down on her."

"You wanted to?"

"Of course I did. I was... I mean, I wouldn't say I was *obsessed* with it, but it was something I wanted, partly because I would get these mouth sores and—well. You don't need the nasty details. But basically, it was something I couldn't have done even if I'd been up for it, and that made me... you know. Want it more." I sighed. "I was so into it. When I was getting to the end of my treatments, I'd look up techniques and stuff online to learn how to do it right."

She giggled, which made me glance up.

"That was your excuse to watch porn?" she asked. "Research?"

I laughed. "I didn't need an excuse, trust me. But I, uh, definitely got a little 'hands-on' during some of my education."

She threw her head back as she laughed and I couldn't help but grin, though it faded as I thought about the next thing I had to tell her.

"Well, anyway, spoiler alert, but I eventually beat the cancer that time, too," I said. "And once I got better, Amanda and I decided we were going to finally hook up. We were about twenty at that point but of course, I was still living with my parents. Not that it mattered, because again—I was the fuckin' sick kid that no one said no to. And I was twenty and horny. So she just came over one night and we went up to my room to fuck while my parents were down in the kitchen." I looked up at her again. "The epitome of romance, I know."

She smiled. "Romance is what you make of it."

"I didn't make much of it," I admitted, looking away from her. "I was just super excited to get my mouth on her pussy. So we're up in my room, we're making out, I get her naked, and I go to go down on her, and..."

I stopped. I had to. My stomach curled again at the memory of that night, the nausea rushing through me so strongly that my mouth watered.

"What happened?" Laura asked softly.

"I puked on her."

From the corner of my eye, I saw her mouth drop open. "What?"

I nodded, heat rising in my cheeks as I thought about it. "When I got down there, I started, um... licking. But I just..." I lifted my hand, rubbing the bridge of my nose as embarrassment washed over me. "There was nothing wrong with her. At all. But when you go through chemo, it can fuck shit up. Like your sense of smell. And taste. Like, when I was a kid, I used to love ranch dressing. On veggies, salad, dipping breadsticks, whatever. Ranch was where it was at. After the first time I went through chemo, though?" I made a face. "It's not as bad now, but I still have a hard time eating it."

"Oh," she said as she began to understand.

"I didn't think that... you know. Pussy would be one of the things I'd start hating," I said. "When I'd done it before, I hadn't been particularly good at it, but it wasn't *bad* as far as the taste went. But with how sensitive everything was after my treatments, it just overwhelmed me and I was so shocked that I just... I couldn't hold it in."

I cringed again, shaking my head.

"So then I'm trying to apologize, trying to clean her up, feeling like a piece of shit as she starts to cry because she's like, 'Oh, my pussy was so gross it made a guy *throw up*,' and I'm trying to explain that's not what happened and it was just a fucking mess, Laura. It was so bad."

I sighed and shook my head.

"She didn't break up with me right away. Said she thought maybe I could try again and, like, desensitize myself. And I was just like... there was no way, you know? I couldn't put either of us through that. So a couple of weeks later, she said she couldn't do it anymore." I smiled, though it was bitter. "She could handle being with me when I was sick, but not when I couldn't go down on her."

"I'm so sorry," Laura said.

I shrugged. "It sucked. So that was... I dunno. That was part of why I started going out and partying and shit. I'd missed out on doing it with my friends because I'd been in treatments. Then I'd lost the girl who spent all that time next to me. I didn't know how to be independent and I didn't care. When you and I met the first time a couple years ago, that was where I was. That's why I... why we didn't keep in touch."

"What?"

I glanced up at her, hoping she could see the apology in my eyes. "That one-night stand? It was fucking amazing. But I would have been an awful person for you to be with then, even if we'd managed to make it work with the different towns and stuff."

"But you wanted to?" she asked. "Be... together? Even then?"

I nodded. "When I saw you in the grocery store that day, I knew it was the second chance I didn't deserve and that I had to get my shit together. I want to be the right guy for you, Laura. Always. And then when... today. All of that." I looked down, my eyes stinging in a way I couldn't allow myself to let her see. "If I lost you over this, I'd never fucking forgive myself. So I thought I'd... try."

"You weren't, um... worried?" she asked delicately. "That you might...?"

I laughed, but the sound was watery. "I've got way better control now. And it's not like it would be unexpected."

She didn't say anything in response, just sat up slightly so she could reach forward and take my hand in hers.

"I'm sorry, baby," I whispered.

"Don't be," she replied, then squeezed my hand. "I know you must have a good reason for not wanting to tell me about... you know. Being sick."

I tried to smile as I squeezed her hand back. "Because if you don't know about it, you can't treat me any differently. And I just..." I sighed, looking up at her. "That defined my life for almost a decade. I was the kid who had cancer. And then *just* as I started getting away from that, I got cancer again. But even trying to get past it, it fucks with my life. I just want to show you how much I fucking lov—"

I choked back the word, but it was too late.

"Seth?" she whispered. "Did you—"

I closed my eyes, grimacing. I had to be the least fucking romantic person alive.

"This was *not* how I wanted the first time I said it to go. I wanted to... I dunno. At least bring you flowers or something."

The mattress shifted and suddenly Laura was pulling herself into my lap. When I opened my eyes, her face was directly in front of mine, and her eyes were watering.

"You already show me how you feel," she said. "I already know."

I half-laughed, my throat tight. "I love you, Laura."

"I love you too, Seth."

CHAPTER TWENTY-FOUR
Seth

IT MAY NOT HAVE been the way I wanted to tell her, but that was okay. She still leaned forward and kissed me, and she still wanted me, and she let me hold her close and indulge in the warmth and comfort of her arms. I kept one arm around her waist, holding her in place so she didn't slide backwards off my knees, and brought the other up to her face, brushing her hair off her cheek as I lost myself to her lips.

"Baby?" I murmured after we'd been making out for a while.

"Mmm?" came the dreamy response.

"I still want to try doing it."

She opened her eyes and studied me. "Are you sure?"

I nodded. "Just... just let me see if it's still... you know."

"Gross?" she said helpfully.

"It's not gross," I protested.

She giggled and brushed her lips against mine. "If you really, really want to. And you're at least, like, sixty percent sure you won't puke on me."

"I'd say it's closer to seventy. Maybe seventy-five." I swallowed nervously. "Please don't be mad at me if I still don't like it, though."

"I promise," she said, then ran her fingers through my hair. "I know that's a normal thing that happens after chemo, Seth. My grandma couldn't eat black jellybeans after she had cancer, and she was one of those weird people who loved them."

I half-laughed. "Chemo improved her taste, then."

She giggled. "And even if it wasn't, even if you just *didn't* like going down on me, that would be okay too. Okay? I want you to know that."

Somehow, even though she'd maintained that point of view the entire time, hearing her say it just then was the comfort I needed.

"Okay," I said, then kissed her one more time before making her shriek with laughter as I leaned forward, slowly dropping her to the bed on her back.

Once she was there, I couldn't stop smiling. Nervous as I was, it was like a weight had been lifted. I kissed her breasts again, then ran my hands along her outer thighs and hips before pushing her legs up so I could pull off the tiny panties she was wearing beneath the flannel pajama shirt.

Then, after putting her legs back down on either side of me, I stared at her pussy.

It wasn't like I'd never seen it before. But knowing I was about to put my mouth there made for a different perspective. Laura had a beautiful pussy, with thick lips and a pretty little hole that was still slick with her juices. I waited, worried my stomach might turn again as I thought about licking her, but it didn't.

Which was my first sign that it was all in my head.

Not *all* of it. I mean, the aversion to licking pussy had been a very real thing. And the fact that chemo changed my sense of smell and taste was also very real. But something I hadn't thought to consider was time.

Because yeah, I'd loved ranch dressing as a kid and hated it after chemo, and yeah, I still didn't *love* ranch dressing... but I didn't despise it the way I used to. Most of my distaste for it was based on memories of putting something I used to enjoy in my mouth and having it taste completely different from what I'd expected.

"Would it help if I wasn't watching?" Laura asked when I hesitated, still staring at her pussy as I waited for the nausea that wasn't coming.

I frowned, then tilted my head to the side thoughtfully.

"Then you don't have to worry about making a face or something," she said. "I wouldn't be mad anyway—I mean, I know it's nothing personal—but this way you can be sure of it."

Which was true. So I nodded and she lifted her hands to her eyes, covering them as she waited for me to taste her.

I swallowed hard, then put a shaking hand on each of her thighs before lowering my head. My breath was coming in short puffs through my nose, but even as I drew closer, I couldn't... you know. *Smell* anything. It wasn't until I was in licking distance—literally at a point where I could have stuck my tongue out and tasted her pussy—that I noticed a scent of any kind, and it wasn't an unpleasant scent. She just smelled clean. There was a slight saltiness to it, something very natural and mild, and I frowned.

Amanda's scent had been *much* stronger. Or it had seemed much stronger. Or maybe I just remembered it that way. Suddenly, I wasn't really sure which.

I leaned in closer, then closer, then my lips were pressed against Laura's mound. She shifted, but didn't move her hands away from her eyes. I knew that because even as I poked my tongue out of my mouth and took a small, tentative lap at her folds, I was looking at her to see if she was watching.

It was only as the flavour of her filled my mouth that I looked away, my mind swirling with confusion.

It didn't taste bad, which was good. It didn't taste like much of anything. I'd expected something tangy or musky or salty, but there was no distinctive flavour that stood out or overwhelmed me. Frowning, I lapped at her again, then again, dragging my tongue along her slit until she moved her hips and *moaned*.

"Seth?" she whimpered.

I looked up at her. "Hmm?"

She moved her hands off her eyes, then looked down to see me with my head still between her legs. "Is this okay?"

"Yes," I said, punctuating the word by sticking my tongue out again.

She giggled. "Good. Because it feels... well. Really good."

I couldn't stop smiling.

I tried to since it made licking her a pain in the ass, but I was elated. She reached down, winding her fingers through my hair as she moaned and ground her clit against my tongue. I lavished the little bud with attention, trying to remember all the things I'd "researched" when I'd wanted to do this before. I alternated between licking her pussy and sucking her clit, getting into the feel of her skin and the noises she made when I did something she liked. And I almost couldn't believe it, but my cock started getting hard. My fucking *cock* got hard as I indulged in her, finally doing something I'd resisted for years because I was so scared of someone reacting the same way my ex reacted.

It was a goddamn Christmas miracle.

We talked about it after, me and Laura. About how so many things could affect the way a woman tasted; everything from her diet to medications to what day of the month it was. I mean, she taught biology and shit, so she had a better understanding of it than I did, but it made sense. I still assumed what had happened with Amanda was based on me being just a few months out of chemo and not anything about her hygiene or what she ate or anything, but it was reassuring to know that if things seemed to change, that was normal.

But just then, it didn't matter.

What mattered was making Laura come on my tongue, which I did.

Because that was what I'd always wanted. That was what my obsession had been when I'd wanted to eat a woman out so badly. I wanted to feel her clamp onto my head, to experience the way her pussy would tighten around my fingers, to listen to the cries of bliss as she arched her back and trembled around me.

And God, it was fucking amazing.

It almost felt as good as Laura sitting up when she finished and practically tearing my clothes off before pushing me onto my back. Almost, because once she'd done that, it was her turn to kneel between my knees and take my cock in her mouth. And it was while she was bobbing her head on my cock that I reached down to cup my hand around one of her giant breasts, groaning in appreciation at the feel of her hard nipple pressed into my palm.

"Your tits are so beautiful, baby," I mumbled as she sucked me, her gorgeous eyes locked on mine. "I love them so much."

She moved her mouth up my shaft slowly, releasing my tip with a loud 'pop' before wiping her lips.

"How much do you love them?" she asked.

I smiled, despite the fact that my cock was no longer in her hot, wet mouth. "Completely."

"Enough to fuck them?"

I almost came on her out of sheer surprise. "You'd let me do that?"

Her pretty lips curled up into a roguish smile. "I'm surprised you haven't already asked, to be honest with you."

So that was how I ended up with Laura's tits surrounding my cock, holding myself back as I thrust between them and then completely losing it when she bowed her head and took the tip in her mouth.

"Gonna come," I grunted, and she released the head of my cock and started moving her breasts up and down just in time for me to watch ropes of cum splatter her chin and neck and chest.

And honestly, she looked so fucking hot with my cum dripping off of her that I... well.

I fucked her like that. And didn't stop until I came again, which was after she'd come twice more.

What could I say? I was in bed with the most beautiful woman in the world, a woman who loved me and who I loved back, who accepted me, forgave me for my faults, and let me literally *fuck* her *tits*.

My cock didn't even have a chance to consider going soft before I was ready to fuck her again.

When we finally finished and I'd stumbled to her bathroom to get a towel to clean us up, it was too late for me to bother going back to my place. Instead, I curled up in bed with Laura naked in my arms, my heart full and my mind blissfully empty.

"I think we're on the naughty list," Laura mumbled out of nowhere.

"Huh?" I asked, already half-asleep.

"The shelf elf," she said. "He spies on people and reports back to Santa and I'm pretty sure Santa would consider the things you did to me tonight firmly on the naughty list."

"That's okay, baby." I yawned and snuggled in closer. "You don't need a gift from Santa. He'd just bring you something cheap and stupid, and I already gave you a pearl necklace."

She slapped me on the arm, but we were both laughing so hard it was a while before we got to sleep.

CHAPTER TWENTY-FIVE

Phoebe

I SHOULD JUST TAKE it off.

That's what I kept telling myself.

Take it off. Crumple it in a ball. Shove it back in the stupid muted pink bag it had come in, put the bag in one of the eighty bajillion purses I owned, and tuck that purse into the back of our closet. Then in January, when Miguel insisted we start the new year by clearing out the clutter and miscellany of the previous year, put that purse in a garbage bag to donate to the thrift store in Calgary. No one would be the wiser.

Except for whatever poor sap opened the purse and found a bag containing wrinkled red lingerie, leading them to wonder with mild disgust if it was unworn or not.

I clenched my jaw and closed my eyes, taking a deep breath in through my nose and letting it puff out through my mouth before opening it again.

"Why did I buy this?"

The mouth of the girl in the mirror moved in sync with mine as I whispered my lament yet again. Lingerie was *not* my thing. I'd told Olivia that countless times in the past. Every time Lacy Pleasures had a sale, she wanted me to buy something, and I'd decline. Or she'd end up with an extra-special-super-savings card and try to pass it off to me, and I'd tell her where to shove it.

Politely, of course.

Lingerie was *her* thing. My older sister had always been obsessed with pretty stuff. She was the one who'd loved makeup and hair and sparkles while growing up. The one who had multiple boyfriends, who got drinks bought for her every time she was at Whiskey Sours, and who loved me probably far more than most older sisters loved their younger sisters.

We'd never fought growing up. Or, well, hardly ever. I supposed every set of siblings have a few fights, but ours were few and far between. Instead of tagging along and annoying her and her friends, I was usually buried in a book, and Liv would come drag me out of my room to play with her. She included me in everything, making a point of ensuring I felt welcome and wanted and... well... loved.

I had an awesome sister.

But try as she might, I was always destined to be the introverted one. Liv was tall and outgoing; I was short and shy. She would pull me into her room and do my makeup as she chattered about boys and music and movies; I would try to explain the plot of the latest book I'd read, which I never seemed to do a very good job of.

She would always listen like I was saying the most interesting thing in the world, though.

Even as adults, Liv tried to pull me out of my shell. And sometimes, she succeeded. Like when we'd gone to Whiskey Sours a few years earlier and she saw me drooling over the hot bartender mixing our drinks. I'd never be able to truly thank her enough for hyping me up and plying me with the exact number of margaritas I needed to approach the bartender without making an ass of myself. Because if she hadn't, Miguel would have never asked for my number, and I would've missed out on the passionate, tender, caring man that was the love of my life.

Miguel.

I stared at myself in the full-length mirror in our bedroom closet, heat crawling up my chest and neck. I was ass-over-teakettle in love with that man. And he... well.

He was probably neck-in-neck with Olivia when it came to which of them loved me more.

In different ways, of course.

Because Miguel definitely did *not* see me as a sister. I stifled a laugh at the thought, pressing my lips together as I examined the lingerie I was wearing for the bajillionth time.

Before him, I'd only had a couple of boyfriends and Liv, despite being the main person in my life urging me to date, had hated all of them.

"You deserve better," she would tell me as soon as whoever I brought home to introduce to my family for the first time was gone.

"What's wrong with *Insert-Whatever-His-Name-Was-Here*?!" I would ask.

She would fold her arms across her chest, anger and hurt flashing across her face. "He just doesn't treat you the way you deserve."

"He treats me wonderfully."

"Every woman deserves a man who worships her," she would say.

And I didn't know what that actually meant until I met Miguel.

I didn't know what it was like to be with someone who loved me for how I looked, not in spite of it.

Growing up, I'd always been chubby. For years, I tried every diet I could think of. I tried working out. I would go out for dinner and then come home and sob, wondering why all my friends could eat an appetizer *and* an entree *and* a dessert without ever seeming to gain a pound, and I couldn't eat one without feeling it pile onto my hips and belly and ass. Liv would try to tell me that there was nothing wrong with my weight, that it was okay to be curvy, and I tried to believe her.

I tried.

But the world isn't always as nice as your sister is, you know?

It wasn't until I was in my early twenties that a doctor finally believed me when I brought my food journal in and broke down in tears, explaining how hard I was trying to lose the weight they kept telling me I needed to lose. It wasn't until then that they tested my hormones and did some scans and told me I had PCOS, and that was why I'd always had a hard time losing weight. With a bit of medication and guidance, I started to see some results, but the chances of me ever being *thin* were...

Well, close to zero. Especially when I said that enough was enough, that I shouldn't have to spend so much of my time dieting and exercising how I was, even with the medication. Liv had celebrated that day because she'd been trying to tell me that for years, but it's a lot easier to say those kinds of things in a normal-sized body like she was.

I'd never quite gotten to a point where I loved my body. I was smaller than I used to be thanks to the medication regulating my hormones and all that, but there were still years of horrible thoughts stemming from the horrible words people said about me to undo.

But I was at the point where I didn't *hate* my body. And that was progress. It wasn't perfect, but it was a lot less painful than it was to despise how I looked.

Miguel, on the other hand, loved my body. He loved it now as much as he had when it was a little bigger, before the medication had helped me go down a few sizes. He loved it when I wore jeans, and even more when I wore skirts, and when I was naked... whew. I'd never had someone look at me the way he did, like I was perfection personified.

Like he couldn't get enough of me.

It astounded me some days, honestly. Miguel was... I didn't even know if there was a strong enough word to describe how phenomenal he was. He was born in Brazil, but his family had moved here when he was a kid. So while his parents had strong accents, he didn't speak with much of one unless he was talking to them, usually in Portuguese. He had warm brown skin, sparkling brown eyes, and a wide nose that I absolutely adored. His hair was a bit curly on top, but he kept the sides cut short, and he usually had neatly trimmed scruff on his cheeks and chin. Add in strong arms and a broad chest and just the *nicest* ass you've ever seen on any guy ever, and that was Miguel.

That was my man.

My perfect, gorgeous, absolute panty-dropper of a man. On my more self-conscious days, I marvelled at the fact that someone as beautiful as him was with me. Not that I ever said that out loud; Miguel would have hated hearing it.

Miguel would have hated hearing the thoughts I was having just then, too.

I bit my lip. The girl in the mirror did, too, and mimicked me as I brushed my long, black hair over my shoulder. Part of me could understand that I was arguably not *unattractive*. I did have nice skin and pretty eyes and shiny hair. And my body was... was...

I grimaced.

I wanted to say my body was beautiful. That my hips were wide and soft and curvy. That my ass might have been on the larger side, but it was round and perky. Or that my breasts had a lovely shape and big, pretty nipples and enticing cleavage. And that the red babydoll-and-thong lingerie set I'd let Olivia and Candice and Trish talk me into buying looked amazing. I wanted to tell myself it contrasted both my hair and my skin, and when I added the pink lipstick I'd smeared on before standing in front of the mirror, I almost looked like a naughty version of Snow White or something.

But when I looked in that mirror, what I saw was dimples on my thighs. Stretch marks on my ass. Breasts that were too saggy for someone who was only twenty-seven. And that belly.

Always that belly.

"I should just take it off," I said to myself.

But I didn't want to.

I wanted to wear it for Miguel. I wanted to feel pretty and desirable. I wanted all of the contradictory feelings to go away. Wear it because I wanted to look sexy. Not wear it because I doubted I could. Keep it on and tell those intrusive thoughts where to stick it. Give in and take it off and go back to the comfortable flannel plaid pajama pants and racerback tank top I usually wore to bed.

How one person had the capacity to feel so many opposing things at once was beyond me, but overachiever that I was, I somehow managed.

I swallowed, trying to soothe my dry throat. This was something I could do. Miguel loved me and my body. It didn't matter that I was only seeing stretch marks and rolls; he would see something entirely different. And he was going to be home soon. He'd texted me to say he was just finishing up his closing tasks and that he'd be on his way. Then I could just seductively walk out of the bedroom and go up to him in the kitchen and—

"Nope," I said, then turned on my heel as I started trying to untie the front of the babydoll. "Nope, nope, nope."

This part of my journey to not hate my body could happen another time. One where I hadn't been eating cookies and drinking mimosas all day.

Just as I made the decision, the back door opened with a loud bang.

"Hey, princess!" Miguel called, like he always did, and I froze.

I fucking froze.

CHAPTER TWENTY-SIX

Phoebe

"PHOEBE?" MIGUEL SAID A few moments later when I didn't respond to his greeting.

Fuck.

"Hi!" I said brightly.

"Where are you?" he asked.

His voice was getting closer. I whirled around, catching sight of myself in the mirror. My eyes were wide and startled, my lips parted—and still fucking covered in pink lipstick—and he was going to see me and...

Without thinking, I yanked my bathrobe off a hanger. It clattered to the floor of the closet, but I kicked it under the rack of Miguel's dress shirts and tugged my robe on, just barely managing to get it tied before Miguel's head poked into the bedroom and turned, staring at me standing in the walk-in closet.

"I'm in here," I said.

"I see that," he said, eyebrows creased with amusement. "Any particular reason?"

"Just getting dressed after my shower," I said, which was true. It was just that I'd gotten out of the shower an hour earlier and had been standing in front of the mirror, trying and failing to hype myself up to wear the lingerie for him.

"Hmm," Miguel said, and his eyes trailed down my covered body. "I wasn't fast enough, I guess."

My cheeks flared with warmth and I laughed awkwardly. "You can look later. You need dinner first."

Because he usually worked so late at Whiskey Sours, Miguel didn't eat dinner at the usual time. Most nights, he was home by eleven, but he was more of a night owl than I was. So he'd eat lunch during his break while at work, which would be around the time I'd eat dinner like a normal person. Then I'd pack up the leftovers of whatever I'd made and put them in the fridge for him to eat. If it was during the week, I'd sit with him and talk while he ate, then go to bed. He'd stay up playing video games or watching TV. In the morning before I left for work, he'd wake up to make me coffee and kiss me goodbye, even though he would've only slept for a few hours. Then he'd go back to bed while I went to my job at the library.

I wished our schedules aligned a little more, but we made it work.

"How did the cookie exchange go, princess?" Miguel asked as I followed him to the kitchen.

"Good," I said. "It was, um, fun to see so many people at once."

He burst out laughing. "Seeing people was fun?"

I bit back a smile. He knew how much of an introvert I was. "Well... it wasn't horrible."

"Not horrible is good. And then you came home and turned off your phone so you could recover?"

I smiled, going to the fridge and pulling out the leftover tacos I'd made for him. "Not quite. I went shopping with Candice and Trish."

"Oh yeah? What'd'ja buy?"

My throat tightened, but I tried to laugh. "Nothing."

That did not fool him, even a little bit.

"Nothing at all?" he repeated. "Or... oh."

"Oh, what?" I asked, trying not to sound alarmed at his knowing tone.

"Nothing you can tell me about, right?" He tapped the side of his adorable nose, grinning at me. "Helping out Santa and all that."

A less flustered person would have probably thought of that on their own, but there we were.

"Something like that," I said.

"So that's why you saw Olivia today?"

My shoulders tensed and I looked at him, eyes wide. "How'd you know that?"

"She came by for a drink after work. Said you'd stopped in."

Fuck. What if she'd told him about the lingerie?

"Um. Yeah. We popped into Lacy Pleasures to see Liv and say hello."

"Didn't buy anything?"

I released a breath that I was completely aware I'd been holding, relieved that my sister hadn't informed him of my reluctant impulse buy. "Candice bought some fancy panties and stuff."

"Liv didn't talk you into one of those full-body latex catsuits?"

"Of course not," I said, though my heart had started to pound. "Why? Would you like that?"

He glanced up, a wicked glimmer in his deep brown eyes. "Princess, I love you in—or out of—anything."

Another rush of heat moved up my cheeks. Tearing my eyes away from him, I started opening the containers on the counter.

"Um, so, what about you?" I asked. "How was work?"

He heaved a huge sigh as he grabbed a plate from the cupboard. "It was... weird, I guess?"

"How so?"

"That pre-Christmas weirdness," he said. "Busy but not busy at the same time. And I don't know *what* it was, but Gwen—you know, the blonde server with—"

"She's Liv's roommate," I said. "I know her."

He grinned one of those abashed, apologetic grins that made my heart melt. "Of course you do. Sorry. My brain's still in work mode."

"It's okay. What did Gwen do?"

"She didn't do anything. She was telling me she had this table who, I swear to God, spent the entire night talking about eating pussy."

I almost dropped the entire container of taco meat on the ground.

"R-Really?" I asked. "Just... just out there in public like that?"

"Uh-huh. I didn't believe Gwen at first, but then I glanced over and there's this redheaded dude ducking his head and like—" Miguel stuck his tongue out, then bobbed his head like a chicken, and I couldn't help but giggle. He stopped, grinning at me as he leaned in to steal a kiss. "And Gwen said they were talking about it each time she went up to ask if they needed more drinks."

"Did you know who they were?" My voice came out dry and I cleared my throat.

Miguel shrugged. "Construction guys or something. They come in now and then but I don't know any of them personally. But Liv went home with one of them."

That time, I did drop a container, but at least it was just lettuce.

"My *sister*?!" I said, eyes wide.

He burst out laughing. "Yeah. One of the guys came back later in the night and hit on her."

"But she... she—" I stared at him. "Was she okay? Did he seem—"

"She was fine." He put down the plate he'd taken from the cupboard, pulling me into his arms and pressing a kiss to my cheek before letting go so he could start cleaning up the lettuce covering the kitchen floor. "I checked in on her and she said she was good. They went back to her place and left his car at the bar. And I told Gwen if she got home after work and something was wrong to text me."

"Okay," I said. "Good. I... okay. Did he seem nice?"

Miguel shrugged. "I guess. He was the ringleader at the pussy-eating table, apparently. For Liv's sake, hopefully he wasn't just talking out of his ass. She deserves a good guy for once, you know?"

I nodded silently as he put the floor-lettuce into the garbage and took the container of meat to the microwave to heat it up. A table of tradesmen talking about eating pussy... they had to be from Candice's husband's crew. I mean, I guess it was possible that it was unrelated to the question Candice had asked, but what were the chances of that?

And I just...

Candice had guessed correctly when we were at the mall. Before Miguel, I'd been with people who didn't exactly find my body *attractive*. Part of me had always known that. Part of me had always felt uncomfortable when I was naked with them, even though I told myself that was normal, that everyone felt that way, that it was okay to settle people who were "not repulsed by" my body, rather than attracted to it.

It wasn't until I met Miguel that I even realized what good sex was. What it was like to be with someone who wanted you—really *wanted* you—and that I didn't have to feel uncomfortable when I was naked. That someone could feel the way he did about me. But even still, even knowing that Miguel loved every bit of my body and then some, I didn't want him to...

You know.

Lick me there.

He'd brought it up once, early on in our relationship and not too long after we actually started having sex. It was before we'd moved into this house, when he was still living in a rental with a couple of roommates.

And by "brought it up," I didn't mean like it was some big, serious conversation. No, we'd been fooling around in his bed, music playing to drown out the soft creaks of his bed frame as we made out.

I could picture that moment perfectly. Miguel was shirtless, though he still had his jeans on. They were undone and sitting low on his hips, the band of his boxers peeking out of the top. And I was almost naked, clad in just my bra and panties.

He was kneeling between my legs, kissing my neck, the warm skin on his stomach pressed against mine as he held himself over me. And I was running my fingertips along his upper back, sighing as he nibbled his way down to my breasts. Which was fine, because I liked it when he touched my breasts and sucked on my nipples and buried his face between them.

Especially when I could feel his reaction to being nestled against me.

But this time, he didn't pause at my breasts like he normally did. He kissed along my cleavage, then caressed one breast before letting his lips move lower... then lower... then...

"Um," I said when his lips were firmly out of breast territory and closer to belly button territory.

"Hmm?" he said, glancing up as he kissed my belly.

"What... what are you doing?" I asked, my voice squeaky.

A devilish look crossed his eyes, something that in almost any other situation, I would've found irresistible.

"I'm going down on you, princess," he said.

It felt like every muscle in my body tensed at once. "Oh. You don't, um, have to do that."

"Have to?" he repeated. "I *want* to. I wanna taste you and lick you and make you come on my tongue. Don't you want me to spoil you, princess?"

He made it sound so enticing. And I wanted to do anything I could to make him happy, because back then I still had this idea in my head that I needed to give and give and give and never ever take, because before Miguel, my boyfriends had only ever wanted to take from me. So I nodded, even though my spine was so tight it felt like it was going to snap and the thought of what he was about had nearly extinguished the sparking arousal I'd been feeling.

And he believed me, because why wouldn't he?

It wasn't until he'd kissed his way down the rest of my stomach, peeled my panties down, and started exploring me with his tongue that he'd glanced up and realized I had my eyes screwed shut and was clenching his bedsheets in my hand.

"What is it?" he asked, his voice urgent with concern as he sat up. "What's wrong, Phoebe?"

"Nothing," I said quickly. "It's okay. K-Keep going."

"Do you think I'm the kind of monster that would keep going when you're clearly upset?" he asked.

"Of course not," I said, my voice catching. "It's nothing you did wrong, I j-just... I..."

I don't know which of us was more horrified when I started crying. Miguel *said* he wasn't horrified, but I couldn't see how that was true. No one wants the person they're with to start sobbing in the middle of sex, which is what I did. He'd pulled himself up beside me, wrapping his arms around me tight and rubbing my back as he kissed my hair, murmuring quiet apologies that I kept telling him weren't necessary as I tried to explain why I felt so self-conscious.

"I'm sorry," I sniffled as I buried my head against his shoulder.

"You have nothing to be self-conscious about," he said as he held me against his chest. "Phoebe, I promise you, you're the most beautiful woman I've ever seen in my life and I'm okay with having to tell you that until you believe it, too. I adore every inch of you. But I'm not going to pressure you to do something you don't like just because I like it."

"But if you like it..."

"This is not a deal breaker for me, okay?" He untangled one of his arms, bringing it to my chin so he could tilt my head up and meet my eyes with his sincere gaze. "Do I like it? Yes, absolutely. Do I like you more? *Infinitely* more. You doing something that makes you uncomfortable for my sake doesn't make me happy, alright? And one day, if you decide it's something you're ready to try again, then we'll try it then."

But even as much as I'd tried to improve how I felt about myself, that day hadn't come.

I couldn't bring myself to relax enough to let him do it. Even thinking about it that first time, all I could imagine was the view he'd have when he glanced up. A belly and at least three times the amount of chins I usually had, my breasts sagging to the side while he was face-to-pussy with a part of me that I couldn't *see*. A part of me that was blocked by breasts and stomach, that no one aside from medical professionals holding scary-looking metal instruments had seen up close like that.

But that was a long time ago. Years ago. Things had changed so much, and now...

I was kind of curious.

A little.

I mean, all the women today had raved about it. Except Nadia. She'd been on my side, but did my side really qualify as a side if I'd never tried it?

And then there was what Candice said about sitting on a guy's face...

The thought of it made heat rise not just up my cheeks, but deep in my core, something curious and fearful that sparked itself awake. There was a big difference between lying on my back, feeling vulnerable and awkward and like I was being viewed from the worst possible angle, and being on top of someone.

I pictured myself perched on Miguel's face, knees on either side of his head as he stared up at me. In my imagination, it felt sensual. Erotic. Powerful.

In my imagination, I loved how I looked sitting on him like that.

Except I was standing in the kitchen in my bathrobe, so nervous and self-conscious that I couldn't even show him the fucking lingerie I was wearing. How was I supposed to get on top of him, putting my pussy right on his tongue and—

"Princess," Miguel said gently.

I looked up at him, startled. "Sorry, what?"

His forehead creased, concern in his eyes as he studied my face. "What's wrong?"

"Nothing. I just—"

"You were a thousand miles away from me," he said. "Was it something I said?"

"N-No, of course not. You didn't say anything that... I was thinking."

"About Liv?" he asked. "She's fine, princess. I promise. I wouldn't have let her leave with that guy if I thought—"

"No, not that. It was..."

My mouth felt dry. I tried to think back to what Candice had said when we were at the mall. When she'd looked at me after I'd inadvertently insulted her by insulting myself, and her patient face and blunt logic as she made me admit the truth: that she did look phenomenal in the lingerie, and if she did, logic would dictate that I did, too. I pictured her, how confident and joyful and sensual she was, and how... well, how I was almost *jealous* of her.

If I wanted to be like her, I needed to take a step.

"Talk to me, princess," Miguel pleaded. "Is something bothering you?"

My jaw trembled and I licked my lips, then took a shallow breath.

"If I wanted to... I mean, what would... There's this—" I stopped and cleared my throat, looking at a particularly fascinating spot on the cabinets over Miguel's left shoulder. "How would you feel if I wanted to, um, like... *sionyoface*."

He frowned. "What?"

I bit my lip, trying to stop the trembles rushing through my body. "What would you say if I wanted to, um, sit? On your... face?"

CHAPTER
TWENTY-SEVEN
Phoebe

MY VOICE MAY HAVE been quiet and squeaky, but Miguel had heard me loud and clear.

I mean, he didn't ask me to repeat myself and from the corner of my eye, I could see him looking in my direction. But he didn't respond. When the silence dragged on to a point where I couldn't stand it, I forced my eyes away from the super interesting spot on the cabinet.

His face was almost neutral. Almost blank. His eyes were wide and his mouth set in a straight line. As I met his gaze, he blinked twice, but still said nothing. Aside from the sound of my heart thumping in my ears, hard enough that I was sure that he could see my pulse throbbing at the base of my neck, the kitchen was completely silent.

Then the microwave dinged to let us know the taco meat was ready.

"Or not," I said, trying to make my voice sound casual and conversational as I reached towards the microwave. "It was just a—"

Before I'd even opened the door an inch, Miguel's arm shot out between me and the microwave, firmly slamming it closed. Then, without a word, he grabbed my still-extended hand and led me to the living room. I frowned in confusion as he let go of me and, with a purposeful look, lowered himself to the floor next to the Christmas tree and lay down on his back with his head almost touching some of the presents sitting under the tree.

"Come here, princess," he said.

"What... what are you doing?" I asked, not sure if I was trying not to laugh or cry.

"Getting under the tree."

"Why?"

He turned his head so he could look at me. "Because this is where all the gifts are, and you are giving me a fucking present, Phoebe."

I pressed my lips together, but it wasn't enough to stifle the nervous laugh that bubbled out of my chest. "So... so you would say yes?"

"Is that what you want to hear?" he asked. "Yes. *Sim*. Please. *Por favor*. S'il... how do you say it in French? *S'il vous plaît*. Come here and sit on my face. *Please*."

"You're not scared I'm going to... I don't know. Smother you or something?"

Miguel raised his eyebrows, then propped himself up on his elbows so I could see just how serious he was.

"Listen to me," he said. "If they put me in jail tomorrow and told me I had to pick a way to get executed, you sitting on my face and smothering me would be the top choice. But do you really think you could do that? You think I'm not strong enough to make you move *exactly* where I want you to be?"

That warm place in my core began to tingle. "I... I just thought—"

"You thought wrong," he said bluntly. "Now take off that ridiculous bathrobe and sit on my goddamn face, Phoebe."

"What about dinner?" I asked. "You haven't eaten yet."

A slow smirk spread across his face. "I'm about to, my dear."

In spite of myself, I laughed. "I meant the tacos."

"You're right." He beckoned me towards him. "I'll take your taco delivered directly to my face please, princess."

I couldn't help but giggle, which made him grin. "I walked into that, didn't I?"

"You did." He licked his lips. "And after all that walking, I think you deserve to take a seat, don't you?"

Oh, God.

Was I really doing this?

I was, I told myself. If I wanted to stop, Miguel would stop. I mean, he wouldn't even have to stop; I would just... just stand up.

And it would be fine. So would the lingerie. He'd like that and I looked fine and there was nothing for me to worry about at all, even though my entire brain was screaming at me to worry and—

"Please, Phoebe," Miguel said softly, the playful demands gone from his voice as it took on a pleading, desperate tone. "I want you like this so badly."

And just...

I was doing this.

My fingers trembled as I brought them to the belt of my robe and worked the knot loose. I could feel him watching, the sensation of his gaze almost palpable. Then, once my robe was undone and the only thing holding it together was my own hands, I took a breath to steady myself—in through my nose, out through my mouth—and let it fall open, shrugging it off my shoulders in one fluid movement.

There was a beat of silence where I couldn't bring myself to look up. Then:

"Holy *fuck*," Miguel said.

I glanced up. He was still resting on his elbows, but his eyes were as round as the ornaments on the tree and his lips were parted as he stared. Licking my lips, I watched as his eyes trailed down my body, part of me itching to hunch forward and cover myself up.

But a bigger part of me—a part that had a voice that suspiciously and slightly alarmingly sounded like Candice's—told me to let him eat his heart out because he wasn't looking at me like I was his princess.

He was looking at me like I was his fucking *queen*.

"Phoebe," he whispered, his eyes finally reaching mine. "Is this a dream?"

I almost giggled, but when I opened my mouth, something completely unlike me slipped out instead.

"Come over here and find out," I said, and before I could even process how I'd *thought* of something like that, Miguel had scrambled to his knees and crawled forward, stopping when he was kneeling at my feet with his neck craned up to look at me.

Without so much as a glance down, he let the fingers of one hand brush against my ankle. When I didn't disappear and he didn't wake up from the dream he thought he might be having, he brought his other hand to the other ankle.

"Princess," he breathed, and then his hands began to move.

His fingertips skimmed along my skin, feather-light and tantalizingly tender as he traced a path up the outside of each of my legs. From ankle to calves, calves to knees, then a slight pause as he twisted his wrists so his fingers were pointed up and he could flatten his palm against my skin. He moved his hands up higher, leaving a scorching path behind as he caressed the outside of my thighs all the way up to my hips.

"Look at you," he said as he slipped his hands beneath the flowy fabric of the babydoll chemise. "Jesus Christ, princess. Was I really so good this year that I get my Christmas gift a week early?"

His fingers reached the waistband of the lacy red thong as he spoke and he traced one fingertip along the silky fabric, dragging it across the band overtop of my belly before flattening his palm again so he could caress my stomach. My breath hitched as he touched me there, as he worshiped that part of me that I'd always stared at with despair, like it was the most beautiful thing in the world.

"You think I'm your gift?" I asked.

"You always are and always have been my present, princess. Just like you will always be my future." He kissed my stomach, gripping my sides so he could guide me forward and nuzzle against me as he stared up into my eyes. "There's not another gift in this entire world or this entire lifetime that I want the way I want you, Phoebe."

God, he was good with his mouth.

In more ways than one, I was discovering. He peppered kisses everywhere he could reach on my stomach, above the fabric and along my skin in places the flowing gauzy fabric of the babydoll chemise hung open. And along the front of the lacy red thong, the fabric so insubstantial it felt like he was kissing bare skin there, too. His hands traced my curves, running along my sides and hips, skimming along the exposed skin on my ass and cupping my ass cheeks gently.

He gazed up at me with those dark, deep, filled-entirely-with-love eyes of his for a while, then let them flutter closed as he exhaled a sigh that was full of need. His hands wrapped around me, palms on my ass cheeks to urge my hips forward against his face. He pressed a kiss just below my belly button, then slightly lower, and lower still.

"Do you know how much I've wanted to taste you again?" he murmured, his lips brushing against me.

I wasn't sure if he meant to say it or even for me to hear it, but I made a soft noise in acknowledgement. Miguel's mouth twisted up into a smile that I felt and he kissed my mound again, his lips just above my clit. His next kiss landed on my slit, his nose pressing into my panties. He paused, inhaling deeply, then exhaled with a groan.

"Fucking amazing," he muttered.

One of his hands left my ass, tracing along the leg hole of the thong. The hem of the chemise brushed against his hand, then tangled slightly around his wrist. Patiently, he shook it off, then again a moment later when it did the same thing.

Once that hand reached the front of my panties, he looked up at me again, holding my gaze as he slipped his fingers into the crotch of the thong and slowly—*agonizingly* slowly—peeled it away from my pussy. My body tingled with electric anticipation, enough that my nipples hardened beneath the lingerie and I was sure Miguel could see them through the fabric.

If he'd been looking, I mean.

He wasn't, though. He was looking into my eyes, even as he bared my pussy just inches from his face. Even once the thong was pushed to the side, he kept his eyes on mine, his expression soothing and calm and earnest.

"Phoebe," he said, and I could feel his words on his breath, brushing against my slick pussy lips. "Princess, you're sure this is what you want?"

I swallowed back the instinctive fears and nodded.

"You're *sure*?" he pressed. "The worst day of my life was the day I made you uncomfortable, intentional or not. I won't repeat it."

I felt like he was being a little dramatic—I was sure he'd had far worse days, though I could understand why his girlfriend stopping in the middle of sex because she started crying was definitely on the list of *bad* days—but his passion and consideration were some of the many reasons that I loved him. Even if I'd wanted to, I couldn't have stopped the smile that spread across my lips.

"I'm sure," I said, my voice soft but sincere. "I want to at least try, Miguel. But I thought..."

"Thought what?"

I could feel my face turning red. "That, um, you wanted me to... you know. You were lying on the ground."

He smirked, the corners of his eyes crinkling.

"I do. But it's only proper to kneel and worship my queen before she takes a seat on her throne."

And oh, God.

Oh *God*.

He was still smiling when he leaned forward and pressed his lips against mine—my pussy lips, that is. I inhaled sharply, but his eyes were full of comfort and devotion and so many good things that I couldn't have felt anything but adored.

With his lips still on my mound, his tongue flicked out, tasting the wetness coating my pussy. I bit my lip as a shiver ran through me, a tremble that radiated from my core up my spine and down my legs, obvious enough that Miguel felt it. He flicked an eyebrow up and I shook my head.

"Keep going," I said breathlessly. "Please."

He looked away from me, glancing down as he traced my folds with his tongue. A moment later, he shifted, pulling the fabric of the thong further away from my slit so he had better access to it. I murmured softly as the tip of his tongue brushed against my clit, enraptured by the sight of him kneeling in front of me.

A few moments after that, he stopped to move the hem of the chemise out of the way. He'd barely resumed licking me when he pulled at the crotch of the thong again, then made a soft, incomprehensible noise.

"This set is beautiful, Phoebe," he said. "Was it expensive?"

"Not overly," I replied, confused. "Liv gave me her discount code."

"Good."

Before I knew what was happening, his hand left my ass and there was a ripping sound. Suddenly, the thong was hanging around my right thigh like some kind of makeshift garter, the left leg hole having been torn in two at the waistband.

"You just ripped my panties off," I gasped.

Miguel looked up, a mischievous glint in his eyes as he tugged the destroyed thong down my thigh so it was out of the way. "You look phenomenal, princess, but I needed better access. Tell Liv to order you another pair."

Then he grabbed my ass again, buried his face against my mound, and started *devouring* me.

CHAPTER TWENTY-EIGHT

Phoebe

I CRIED OUT AS Miguel's tongue found my clit, lavishing it with attention as he made out with my pussy.

There was no build up, no teasing, no gentle kisses here and there to get me worked up. There was no need for any of that; between the adrenaline and the nerves and the beautiful words spilling from my boyfriend's mouth, I'd been *more* than turned on. So instead, Miguel set to work, his mouth making wet sounds as he indulged in something I hadn't been able to give him before that day.

Worship was the word he'd used, and it was the word for it. His hands honoured me and his groans of pleasure were like songs of praise, while his eyes revered me l like I was prized.

Like I was precious.

I moved a shaking hand towards his head, feeling his soft curls beneath my fingertips. One of his wandering hands left its path and found my other hand so he could entwine my fingers in his. Soft noises escaped my mouth as I watched him, my breath quickening as electricity rushed up and down my body.

I was enjoying it. *Me*. Liking what he was doing so much that when he pulled his mouth away a few minutes later, I was disappointed.

Disappointed.

The last time he'd tried going down on me I'd sobbed, and now I wanted more of it.

Maybe my confidence wasn't where I wanted it to be, but that was progress. That was major fucking progress, and I was going to be proud of it.

"It's time, princess," he said, his face glistening as he sat back on his knees. "I can't wait any longer."

A fresh rush of anxiety worked its way through me, but I shook it away. I could do this.

"Okay," I said. "But only if you're sure you want to do this."

He was on his back on the living room floor, unbuttoning the front of his dress shirt, before I even finished speaking, so I guess that answered that.

Once he'd finished undoing his shirt, he extended his arms towards me.

"Come," he said. "Your throne awaits."

I giggled, though it sounded nervous even to my ears as I pushed the torn thong down my right leg so I could step out of it. But I forced myself to move forward, forced myself to work past the feeling of butterflies in my stomach and approach him, the light fabric of the babydoll chemise brushing against my hips.

"So I just, um..." I cleared my throat. "How do you want me to do this?"

Miguel grinned from the floor. "Usually I'd say however you want, but this first time, I'll tell you how I like it, okay?"

"Okay."

He directed me to put a knee on either side of his head, facing away from the rest of his body, and line my pussy up with his chin. Then, as gracefully as I could, I knelt over him, just able to see the top of his head poking out from between my thighs.

"Perfect," he murmured. "Now lower yourself down, princess."

"How much?"

"As much as you want."

"But I'll crush—"

"You won't crush me. But if I need you to let up a bit, I'll tap you, okay?" He wrapped his arm around my leg so his palm was on the top of my thigh, then patted it against me a few times. "Like this. Just means sit up slightly."

"Okay," I said. "And what do I, um, do?"

"Whatever you want. Stay still. Grind against my tongue. Ride my face." I felt him half-shrug. "Try all of them. The more you experiment, the longer I get to be surrounded by heaven. Now—" he hooked his other arm around my thigh and began pulling me down "—stop teasing me with this beautiful pussy. Take a goddamn seat, Phoebe."

I took a deep breath, let it out, then did it.

He moaned as I did, his arms tightening around me as his tongue slipped between my folds again. For the first bit, I stayed still, getting used to the feeling of his tongue and his mouth, to the sounds and the sensations and the way he was groaning like *he* was the one getting head, not me. He ate me enthusiastically, his head bobbing as he alternated between lapping at my pussy and sucking on my clit. His tongue dipped inside me, swirling around my entrance and making me shiver.

It felt strange at first. I couldn't deny that. My heart was pounding, thrumming in my chest as I worked to keep my breathing steady. But it wasn't long before my breath was coming faster not because of nerves, but because it was feeling *good*.

Good enough that I could tell what kinds of things I liked more than others.

Good enough that when Miguel finished sucking on my clit and returned to using his tongue to lap at me, I rolled my hips forward, seeking out even more friction on my clit.

"Right there," I whispered, though I doubted he could hear me given my thighs were on either side of his head. Not to mention the loud groan he let out as soon as I started to move.

One of his hands left my thigh and snaked up the front of my body, finding my breast and cupping it as I worked myself against his tongue. His thumb brushed against my hard nipple through the fabric of the chemise, spiking enough pleasure through me that I let out an actual moan. That earned me another one of Miguel's irresistible noises, plus the sensation of him shifting beneath me so I could grind on his tongue at a better angle.

And it felt amazing.

It felt phenomenal.

It felt like I was an absolute idiot for spending so long *not* doing this, all because I was nervous about my weight.

But that was the past. Now was the present, and in the future, I wouldn't make the same mistake. In the future, there would be a lot more of this.

In the future, I was going to come on his tongue.

Not that night. As much pleasure as there was soaring through my body, I wasn't there yet. I wasn't quite relaxed enough to give into the sensation of overwhelming feverishness. Not so much because I was nervous, but the multitude of emotions I'd experienced were still sorting themselves out within me.

And that was okay. I'd come a long way in a single night. And I could come a little more, just on his cock or his fingers instead. It would still feel amazing.

When I lifted myself off his face, Miguel gasped for breath, but stretched his neck out so he could look up at me.

"You weren't crushing me," he said.

I stifled a laugh. His eyes were wide and wild, his hair mussed, and his cheeks and chin were positively soaked with my juices.

"I know," I said. "I just don't think I'm going to be able to finish like this."

He frowned. "Something I'm doing?"

"No," I said. "You're amazing. I just want you to... This is going to sound so silly. But I want you to make love to me."

The wildness in his eyes faded as a sweet smile spread across his lips. "Princess, I will always make love to you."

I moved off of him and he sat up, using the sleeve of his dress shirt to wipe the wetness off his face before he reached forward and kissed me.

"You know how I know this isn't a dream?" he said against my lips.

"How?" I asked.

"I couldn't come up with a dream as amazing as this." He nipped at my lower lip. "I love you."

"I love you, too."

He undressed quickly, then took a moment to untie the babydoll chemise and gently set it to the side before guiding me onto my back.

"Wait here," he said. "I gotta go get a condom."

I bit my lip. "Or..."

"Phoebe, are you—"

"I'm on the pill. And you can... you know. Pull out."

He studied me, then gently parted my legs and moved between them before leaning forward to kiss me. His cock pressed against my soaked pussy, hot and throbbing and so hard that I thought he must have been in pain.

"This is the best random early Christmas ever," he murmured, and I giggled as he shifted his hips, sliding his cock up and down my slit a few times before reaching down between us. "You're sure?"

"I'm always sure with you," I said.

He smiled, then the tip of his cock was notched in my entrance and we were both sighing as he slid himself inside me.

It wasn't the first time we'd had sex without a condom. Most of the time, we used them, even though my PCOS meant I'd have a hard time if we ever decided to have kids and I took birth control to help with my hormones. We just didn't want to risk it, knowing that neither of us were ready for that. I didn't know if we ever would be. And that was okay. There was still plenty of time to decide if we'd want to be parents one day.

But now and then, we'd throw that one little piece of our excessive amounts of caution to the wind, usually when we were feeling like this; that is, loving and loved. Cherishing and treasured. When telling him I loved him wasn't enough. When having a part of him literally *inside* me didn't bring us close enough together unless that piece was as naked as we were, his hot and throbbing thickness enveloped by the tight, wet walls of my pussy.

When we were on the floor in the living room, clinging to each other, the twinkling lights of the Christmas tree sparkling above us and paper-wrapped boxes tucked underneath it, and I needed him connected to me wholly and completely.

"You are everything to me, Phoebe," he whispered as he moved inside me. "Everything. I never want to let you go."

"I'll never let go," I murmured, and he groaned as he turned his head, burying it against my neck and thrusting deeper.

It didn't take me long to come. I'd been closer than I thought while I was on his face; the feel of his thick cock stretching my pussy as he reached the deepest parts of me was the push I needed to fall over the edge. When I did, I clutched at him, wrapping my legs around his waist as my whole body shook. Pulses of light flashed in my eyes and waves of bliss took over. I'd barely started to come down when Miguel staggered and groaned desperately.

"Gonna," he stammered. "Princess, your legs…"

It wasn't even a decision; the words spilled out of me and I heard them for the first time as he did.

"It's okay," I said. "Come inside me. I promise it's okay."

"Oh, *God*," he choked. "Are you—"

I assumed the next word was "sure," but he came before he could get it out. I felt his cock twitch as he shoved himself as deep inside me as he could, hot cum spilling out of him as he groaned. I kissed the side of his head and held him close, relishing the feel of him finishing inside me, my mind hazy and satisfied and content beyond words.

We stayed that way for a while, him resting heavily on top of me, our bodies pressed together as we caught our breaths. When he finally shifted and pulled his cock out, I sighed, my eyes still closed as I basked in that fuzzy warm feeling of afterglow.

"I think..." Miguel said, then trailed off.

"Think what?" I asked sleepily.

When he didn't respond, I opened my eyes. He was looking at me, his beautiful dark eyes set with an oddly determined look.

"I think it's only fair if you get an early Christmas present, too," he said.

I laughed, sure I was blushing. "You don't think that counted as a gift for me?"

"No. That was for me and I don't plan on sharing it. I just... I want to." He leaned forward, his body hovering over mine as he reached under the tree and rifled through the presents sitting there. "More than anything, I want to. Right now. Even though..."

He trailed off, his movements stilling for a moment.

"Even though what?" I asked.

He chuckled softly. "Even though you deserve better than this moment. But I can't wait, princess."

A moment later, he withdrew his hand, it was clutched around a small square box wrapped in gold paper. My breath caught in my throat.

"Miguel, I—"

"Open it," he whispered. "Please."

I sat up, completely forgetting I was naked. Completely forgetting he'd just come inside me and it was probably going to get on the carpet. I just sat up, heart racing as I took the small box from him and carefully unwrapped it, taking care not to tear the paper.

I saw the box for all of a second before my vision blurred over with tears. When he took it from me and flipped it open so he could ask that one little question, I couldn't have even said what the ring looked like. But what it looked like didn't matter. It would never matter. It didn't matter that we were both naked, or that we'd have to come up with a far more appropriate story to tell people about how he'd done it.

This was our present and our future.

I loved him, and he loved me, and I said yes.

CHAPTER TWENTY-NINE

Jay

DESPITE HAVING TO WORK Sunday, everyone was oddly cheerful when they got to work the next morning.

One could say they were jolly, even.

"You're late," I said to Seth as he scrambled past me towards the build ten minutes after he was supposed to be there.

"Sorry," he said, his voice hoarse.

I frowned as I studied him. There were dark circles under his eyes and his hair was messy.

"And you look like hell," I said.

He laughed. "Thanks, boss."

"Everything alright?"

"Everything's great. Just, uh... didn't sleep well," he said.

I nodded slowly. "Alright. Don't get hurt because you're too tired to pay attention. The last thing I need today is a worker's comp claim."

"You got it."

When I joined the rest of the crew inside, Benny was whistling as he worked like he was in fucking Snow White.

"What're you so happy about?" I asked.

He shrugged and continued whistling.

"Dunno what you're complaining about, ya damn Scrooge," Adrian said from where he was loitering near the toolbox. "Do you know how hard it was to drag myself out of bed this morning knowing I was giving up a hot, tight—"

"We don't need to hear about your escapades with your Fleshlight," Kendra said.

He gave her an unimpressed look. "I was going to say 'nest of blankets,' pervert. And her *name* is Olivia."

"Your Fleshlight has a name?" Rob asked.

"Excuse you," Adrian said with a laugh. "That's not a very nice way to talk about your neighbour."

"What?" Rob said.

A shit-eating grin spread across Adrian's face. "Your neighbour. Olivia. She lives in your building, on the fourth floor? Nice girl, works at the lingerie store in the mall? But frankly, the fact that you consider women to be nothing more than a Fleshlight is really worrying, my friend."

"Oh, fuck off," Rob said, but he'd started laughing. "How was I supposed to know an actual woman wanted to take your sorry ass home?"

"Wait, so you actually got laid last night?" Kendra asked.

Adrian pretended to examine his nails arrogantly, which was somewhat ineffective given that he had his work gloves on.

"I did," he said. "And not to brag, but I fucking rocked her world so hard she's having dinner with me tonight."

"Wait, *you* have a date?" Benny said as he turned away from the area he'd been working on.

"Sure do."

"She must've been something else to get you to give up your man-whore ways," Seth said.

"She is," Adrian said, and I swear the fucker's voice was almost *dreamy*. "Is it too soon for me to plan a Christmas morning proposal?"

The crew laughed like he was joking, but I was fairly sure there was a hint of seriousness in Adrian's eye.

"I dunno, man," Benny said. "Sounds pretty sus to me. Since when do you see the same woman for more than a one-night-stand?"

"Since I found one whose oral skills meet or exceed my own," Adrian shot back.

"Right, I forgot," Kendra said, laughing. "You're the pussy-eating master."

I might have been imagining it, but I thought Rob and Benny might have exchanged a look just then.

"Reminds me," Rob said casually. "I got something for you in my truck, Adrian. Don't let me forget before we go."

"Aw, you got me a little present?" Adrian said.

"You said I could pay you back with a bottle of bourbon."

Adrian frowned, then his face brightened up. "No *way*?! You actually—"

"Shut up, man."

Benny burst out laughing. "Too funny. I got him a case of beer for the same reason."

"What reason?" Kendra asked, bewildered.

"The vortex?" Adrian said.

"The vortex," Benny and Rob repeated knowingly.

But none of them elaborated. Kendra and Seth both looked confused and I rolled my eyes.

"Enough chitchat. I wanna get out of here at a decent time. Get back to work, you useless tits."

"Back to work would insinuate we'd started working in the first place," Adrian said.

"And I find tits very useful," Seth said.

I laughed.

"Whoa, whoa, whoa," Rob exclaimed. "Was that a laugh? What's got you so fuckin' chipper this morning, Jay?"

"What do you mean, chipper? I have to work with you assholes," I replied.

"He does seem chipper this morning, doesn't he?" Kendra said.

"We haven't hit the first coffee break and he's giggling like a kid on Christmas morning," Seth said. "I'd say the man's downright fuckin' merry."

Which was true.

I *was* merry. And chipper. And cheerful, jolly, joyous. Whatever you wanted to call it. Because when I'd left the site yesterday intent on going for a drink with some of the crew, Candice had sent me one of those particularly naughty photographs and my dick had directed me to head back home post-haste.

And when I got home?

I showered, then went into the bedroom, where my lingerie-clad wife was lying on the bed with her legs spread wide as she read a book.

"Get to work, darling," she said, casually turning a page.

I didn't come up for air until I'd made her come on my tongue three times, which was a personal record. Usually I could only get two out of her before she was demanding my cock.

I didn't leave our bed until I'd had to drag my sorry ass out of it to come to work. Not even for dinner; we'd ordered pizza and tried to fuck before the delivery guy arrived, but Candice was still riding my dick when the doorbell rang. So she'd ordered me to stay where I was, shrugged her bathrobe on, and went to get it, then brought the boxes to our bedroom and set them on the nightstand on her side of the bed.

"Ready to eat?" she'd asked, opening the box and helping herself to a slice.

I'd have preferred for her to keep riding my cock, but if she wanted to stop, I might as well join her. So I started reaching across her to grab a piece, only for her to stop me.

"Ah, ah," she said. "You can have some pizza when you're done *eating*."

And if you think I wasn't going to go to town on my wife's pussy while she ate pizza... well. I guess that means you've missed the point.

But despite having to leave the comfort of my warm bed and my gorgeous sleeping wife to come out here into the fucking cold and bust my ass to finish the job before Christmas, I was in a pretty good mood. Candice had finally convinced me to get up by promising to show me the other things she'd bought from Lacy Pleasures once I got home. Still, I would've much rather spent the day in bed with her, eating cold leftover pizza and some of the cookies from her cookie exchange and watching those stupid Christmas movies she loved so much.

Though, there was a good chance if I saw *The Muppet Christmas Carol* one more time, I might throw up.

Knowing what was waiting for me later made the morning pass slowly, though. There wasn't much chatter as we worked, all of us focused on our tasks so we could get out of here as soon as possible. Just as I was wondering if it would be worth asking the crew to skip our coffee break and keep going, though, something forced us to stop.

"It's time for a break, everyone!" called a familiar voice from outside the build.

I frowned over the noise of our tools. "The fuck?"

"Is that Candice?" Benny asked.

"The ho, ho, hos are here!" yelled someone else, and then there was a swell of feminine laughter. Rob shot up, his eyes wide.

"Halle?" he said, abandoning his task and striding across the building to the entrance.

"Ooh, if that's Halle, I'm going too," Kendra said. "She's hot."

"You're *married*," I said.

"So?" she said, following after Rob. "Melissa thinks she's hot, too. She was bummed she had to miss out on an opportunity to ogle Halle during the cookie exchange yesterday because she was working."

But as it turned out, Melissa was making up for missing out on the cookie exchange that day.

I started laughing when I left the building and saw what was waiting for us. Standing around the frozen mud-and-snow-covered site were the crew's wives and girlfriends. Halle was already in Rob's arms, giggling as she tried not to drop the Tupperware container in her hands. Beside her, Kendra was kissing Melissa, her hand on the belly of her very pregnant wife. Next to her, Denise was waving wildly as everyone pretended we couldn't tell there was a pregnant belly beneath her bulky winter jacket. And Laura, shyly smiling from under the hood of her pink winter jacket as she clutched a huge thermos of coffee.

Then, in the middle of course, the most beautiful woman in the world.

Candice was grinning that confident, knowing grin of hers. Her lips were painted red and she held a container like Halle's as she caught my eye. Without even consciously making the choice, I started towards her, not stopping until she was close enough to kiss.

"What's all this about?" I asked even as I pressed my mouth to hers.

"Mmm," she replied, kissing me before she pulled back. "I thought I'd drop by after bringing some cookies to the mall for Phoebe's sister. I figured you could use a little surprise on your coffee break since you all had to work today. And the others all wanted to come, too."

"A surprise?" I asked.

She held up the container. "Well, we all have, like, eight dozen cookies. We figured we could spare a few. And—" She glanced at the other women, who were all distracted by their respective partners by that point "—I have a special surprise for you."

I raised my eyebrows and she leaned in.

"The set I got today is pink," she whispered. "And I think you should decide how it comes off when you get home tonight."

I groaned softly. "You're killing me, beautiful."

She laughed, a bright, joyous sound, and parted from me.

"Merry Christmas, everyone!" she called. "We thought you could use a sugar rush to get through the rest of the day."

"Do I get a kiss, too?" Adrian said to Candice as he came up behind me.

"Unless you want to eat these cookies by me shoving them up your ass with my steel-toes, no," I snapped.

He clapped me on the shoulder as both he and Candice laughed. She hugged him hello, but he made the very smart decision to keep his lips to himself.

"I brought you a little extra something, Adrian," she said as we walked over to Rob's truck since he'd volunteered to use the tailgate as a table for the cookies and coffee. "Since all the others got to see their girls."

He grinned as she handed him a small paper bag, which I figured had a mickey of bourbon in it.

"Damn, am I ever going to have a party tonight," he said, tucking it into his coverall pocket. "But maybe next year you'll have someone to invite to this."

Candice's eyes widened. "You met someone? Oh, if I'd known, I would've asked her—"

"Don't worry about it," Kendra said as she helped herself to some cookies and a cup of coffee from the thermos. "He only met her last night."

"And he's already planning the wedding," Benny said as he filled up a coffee cup and handed it to Denise. "All morning it's been 'Olivia this' and 'Olivia that' and—"

"Wait, Olivia?" Candice said. "Does she work at the lingerie store in the mall?"

"Yeah!" Adrian said. "That's, uh, her. How do you know her?"

Candice glanced at me, hiding a smirk. "I occasionally shop there."

"Ooo—" Kendra started.

"Shut up," I said stiffly, and the crew burst out laughing.

Candice slipped her arm around my waist, even as she giggled. "That reminds me. I'm sure she won't mind me spilling the beans, but Phoebe—you know, from the cookie exchange? She's Olivia's sister. She got engaged last night!"

"Aw, that's amazing!" Halle said. "I'm so happy for her. She's seeing that bartender from Whiskey Sours, right?"

Candice nodded. "Miguel. Apparently, that little, um, *discussion* we had at the cookie exchange yesterday set something in motion."

Melissa looked intrigued. "What discussion?"

"They were talking about eating pussy," Kendra said loudly. "And whether men do it for their pleasure or their partner's pleasure."

It was a testament to how well everyone there knew each other that no one looked scandalized at the statement. Though, I did glance at Seth, worried he'd have the same uncomfortably embarrassed look on his face that he'd had when we talked about it yesterday. But he was exchanging a knowing glance with Laura, whose cheeks were pink as she hid a smile behind her cookie.

"Exactly," Candice said. "And as it turns out, one thing led to another and Miguel was so... let's say... *delighted* with what things led to that he hauled out the ring box he'd planned to give her on Christmas morning and got her to open it right then and there."

"That's actually adorable," Denise said.

"I guess that one little question did a lot of good," I said.

There was no mistaking it that time; there were a lot of knowing looks exchanged between partners in the beat of tense silence that followed my statement. Laura didn't manage to suppress her giggle and Seth's face went red, but he looked distinctly proud. Denise was grinning as Benny covered his smile by rubbing his chin and Halle was looking up at Rob, her eyes round as he tried to give her a subtle shake of his head. I looked at Candice, who was watching with an amused expression on her face.

"It sure did do a lot of good," Adrian finally said. "At least for me. I mean, you can all ask Olivia about just how good—"

"Rob freakin' rocked it last night," Halle blurted.

"Halle!" he hissed, but it was lost under the roar of laughter as his face turned red.

"Nice," Kendra said.

"So did Seth," Laura added in a quiet voice.

Seth's face also went red, but that might have had more to do with the loud whoop Adrian let out before clapping him on the shoulder.

"Atta boy!" he said, and I was fairly certain everyone was laughing so hard they couldn't breathe.

When things finally calmed down, no one seemed quite sure what to say. The last few chuckles and giggles faded, leaving us standing there in the cold as we took in the strangeness and hilarity of the situation.

"So Candice," Adrian said. "You got any more of those little questions for us?"

And my wife, ever the mischief-maker, grinned.

ACKNOWLEDGMENTS

My books would not be possible without some very special people:

My proof-readers, editors, and beta readers are extraordinary people who I am incredibly grateful to. Special thank you to Jason Caldwell, Nora Fares, and Chasten.

To Paul M, Kevin Matheny, centralsquareguy, KW, AG, PM, N, ED, KJ, MidNyt, RP, Caleb Waters, and all my incredible supporters on Patreon and in my Cheryl's Terrors group - thank you. Your enthusiasm, support, and belief in me means more than I can ever say.

I am lucky enough to be surrounded by friends and family who have read, supported, and encouraged my writing. To all of you, thank you, and I stand by what I said: you're the one who has to look me in the eye if you read something you didn't want to think about me writing! But also, thank you for not making it weird. I am so grateful for the special people in my life.

And finally, to the man I love more every single day: I love you. You're my everything. Thank you for standing with me, encouraging me to follow my dreams, and being my happily ever after.

ABOUT THE AUTHOR

Cheryl Terra writes romantic and adult fiction with drama, sass, and a whole lot of... spice. Emotional and humorous, her books focus on contemporary relationships, inclusive characters, and happily ever afters. Living with her husband in northern Alberta, Canada, Cheryl relies on the heat between her quirky and memorable characters to help keep the gas bill down in the winter.

When she's not writing, Cheryl can be found listening to the same song(s) on repeat for hours at a time, spoiling her pets, keeping way too many house plants alive, and knitting or crocheting.

For more information and to get free books, visit Cheryl's website at **cherylterra.com**

ALSO BY CHERYL TERRA

*Find all of Cheryl's books by visiting **cherylterra.com/stories***

If You Can Series

The Boy Next Door
Kiss Me If You Can
Hold Me If You Can
Keep Me If You Can

The Unicorn Confessions

The Unicorn Confessions
Unicorn For Sale
Death of a Unicorn

Love Across Canada

Get Over It
The Devil Made Me
Runaway
Finding Home

Join The Chaos

Sign up for my newsletter to get a peek into the behind the scenes chaos, news and release info, access to excerpts and freebies, and D pics.

(if you thought I meant anything other than DOG pics, you wonderful, dirty minded angel, you'll fit right in)

Join here: **cherylterra.com/newsletter**